Praise for Jec A. Ballou's Writing

"Hilarious!" –Doris Eraldi, author <u>Settler's Law</u>

"What a fun blog!" –Maria S., equestrian

"In her latest book, <u>Equine Fitness</u>, Jec Ballou has done the impossible; she has produced a "new" book in an industry where almost every imaginable topic has been covered in multiple texts."
–Donna Snyder-Smith, author <u>The All Around Horse & Rider.</u>

"<u>101 Dressage Exercises</u> is an excellent resource…"
–*Chronicle of the Horse*

"Rippin' great stories! Pleasantly cryptic and sardonic."
–Dr. Sherry Ackerman, author <u>Dressage in the Fourth Dimension</u>

"Training tips and masterly guidance make this (<u>101 Dressage</u>) an indispensable reference for all dressage riders." –Horse Books Etc.

"Hooray! This is why riding with Jec is so much fun!"
–Sonia M., equestrian

The Unscheduled Dismount

Also by Jec Aristotle Ballou

The Unscheduled Dismount

And Other Humor from a Life with Horses

Jec Aristotle Ballou

Trafford Publishing
Bloomington, IN

Order this book online at www.trafford.com
or email orders@trafford.com

Most Trafford titles are also available at major online book retailers.

Printed in Victoria, BC, Canada.

ISBN: 978-1-4269-2263-3

*Our mission is to efficiently provide the world's finest, most comprehensive
book publishing service, enabling every author to experience success.
To find out how to publish your book, your way, and have it available
worldwide, visit us online at www.trafford.com*

Trafford rev. 1/10/2010

 www.trafford.com

North America & international
toll-free: 1 888 232 4444 (USA & Canada)
phone: 250 383 6864 ♦ fax: 812 355 4082

Dedication

THIS LITTLE BOOK of humor is dedicated to anyone who has known and loved horses. If we cannot laugh and enjoy our lives with these animals, what is the point? Horses are our teachers, our friends, and in many ways our access to a more pleasant life. Read these stories and smile.

Acknowledgments

To all the horses far and wide—THANK YOU for putting up with us humans, your admiring friends and loyal stewards. Maybe someday soon we'll figure out what the heck we're doing!

A special nod of gratitude to my clients, students, and colleagues: thanks for the inspiration and fodder. And thanks to the friends who encouraged me to follow my laughs and tackle this project: Rachel Anicetti, my mom and dad, Pher Ballou, Naomi Johnston, Siobhan Saunders, Callie Gregg, Doris Eraldi, and Mark Schuerman. Sometimes, a little shove goes a long way. Lastly, thanks to the eager group of readers that frequented my blog where many of these stories first took form.

Contents

Monkey See, Monkey Do

A FEW YEARS AGO, I read with delight about a phenomenon that I've never proven true but nonetheless really like believing. It's the fact that humans are drawn to pets that look like them. This means that your friend with the adorable Jack Russell has a number of Terrier-like traits herself. Maybe she has a short nose or mischievous expression or a stout little body. And your sister-in-law with her overweight Labrador? Chances are good she has the same chunkiness, same droll eyes. She may even walk in the same hip-shuffling manner.

Admittedly, this is pure speculation since I've not yet proven the pet-human resemblance as fact. But it does make for good people- (and pet) watching. I mean, how about the owner of a Hairless Chinese Crested dog? Are we to assume he or she is bald below the neck line? Or what about the ancient crusty-eyed cat that is still clinging to life after 20 years? Does her owner share the same crustiness?

As stated, I have not decided whether my friends' dogs and cats look like them. Even if I had decided this, I probably wouldn't print it publicly. But after a few decades as an equine professional, I *can* assure you that peoples' pets do eventually *act* like them. With enough time, a pet will adopt the behaviors and moods of its owner, for better or for worse. If you doubt this, do yourself a favor and spend a day at your local equestrian facility observing the interactions between horses and owners.

In my daily life as trainer, I regularly witness the horses in my care transform from normally well-behaved into spoiled idiots the moment they hear their owner's car pull into the driveway. Instantly, they are no longer my composed and obedient charges. In the blink of an eye, they morph into ill-behaved hellions. They paw at the walls and toss their head; they pace in circles and kick out at the horse stabled next door to them. It's as if the presence of their owner unleashes a spoiled personality that is otherwise dormant. Likewise, I've witnessed stolid and steadfast mounts turn into spooky freaks once their owners mount up for a ride.

And this of course is my point. Animals will behave in ways that reflect the internal states of their owners—fearful, wound-up, angry, or well-adjusted. The latter, I see rarely in horses and humans alike. Most of us are not nearly as well-adjusted as we prefer to think. Like it or not, our animals mirror us. They take on our neuroses, our strengths, our weaknesses, and everything in between.

Sometimes it's uncanny how resistant we are to admit this. I recall an episode a few years ago where I was riding a client's young mare in the middle of a productive schooling session when the student raced in the driveway, kicking up clouds of dust behind her sports car. She spilled out of her car, eyes bulging from a day of stress at the office, clutching a cell phone in one hand and a large extra-caffeinated mocha from Starbucks in the other. Using the speaker function of her phone, she conducted a conversation with her ex-husband that used volumes of profanity I hadn't heard since high school.

Anyway, before I knew it, she was in the arena with me (having put the ex-husband on mute) and wanted to ride her horse. Mentally, I came up with a dozen immediate reasons why that amounted to a bad idea. Against my better judgment, I gave in and told her she could ride if she would just take five minutes of silence to settle down. To her, that meant finishing her mocha.

Before I knew it, I was giving this stressed-out, hyped-up woman a leg up on her young unsuspecting horse. Needless to say, within moments, the horse mirrored the woman, even without the ingestion of a 16-ounce mocha. It began darting around the arena, jumping out of its skin, and—I'm not kidding—its eyes bulged like its owner's.

The woman wanted to know what was wrong. I gently pointed out that the horse picked up on her frenzied state and was absorbing that energy, causing it to be unsettled. Of course this made no sense to Ms. Starbucks. Horses are horses, she said. As if they are completely dead to sensory input. No, I reminded her, horses are like their owners. She cared little for this comparison and within months took the horse to a progression of other trainers who all told her the same thing.

The fact that horses mirror their owners can actually be a very favorable trait. For example, my trainer friend Mark Schuerman is the calmest, most unflappable person I know. And he imparts that spirit to every horse in his barn. Within two months of life with Mark, horses adopt a serene attitude towards the world. It's like a magical transformation or osmosis of sorts. I was deeply grateful for that one night six years ago shortly after I first moved to California.

I moved my training operation into a vacancy at the barn where Mark was based. At that time he trained exclusively Arabians, an otherwise high-strung breed of horses that became docile puppies under his hand. Being reputable in the Arabian world, he was invited to give a short riding performance at the Western States Horse Expo, the largest horse exposition on the West Coast that regularly attracts 65,000 or more spectators over one weekend in June. Mark was honored. He would ride one of his most prancing, gorgeous, bay Arabs under spotlights in the late-night ticketed show. He agreed to it with enthusiasm.

Then he got a hot date for that same night. But he didn't want to let down his fans from the Arabian community, so he held his commitment to do the Expo gig by recruiting me to ride his horse. I agreed without further thought because, first of all, I had no idea what I had gotten into and secondly, I knew Mark really wanted to go out with his attractive blonde date. So, there you have it.

A few weeks later at the Expo, I found myself at 10:00pm mounted atop an increasingly nervous Arabian gelding squeezed into a crowd of roughly 100 other demonstration riders on equally nervous horses in the pitch black scrambling around on pavement while we each awaited our turn to blast into the main arena for five minutes of glory.

There's much I don't remember about that evening. What I *do* remember is that the act preceding my ride was a mounted shooting demonstration, which meant that while I waited with my snorting Arabian outside the arena's main gate, a dozen or more out-of-control riders galloped around inside shooting pistols at balloons until they all popped. I'm not sure if it was the gunfire, my sudden nausea, or all the yelling and screaming, but my horse was quickly coming unglued.

I tried dialing Mark on my cell phone to tell him not only was I not going into that arena, but this night marked the end of our friendship, too. Before the call went through, though, a rearing Friesian stallion streaked across the pavement towards me, slid on his shoes, and rammed into my horse's backside. That itself would have been startling enough. But the horse and his rider, a wannabe eighteenth century knight, were entirely decked out in chain mail armor. The more the horse reared, the more his armor clanked and rattled, which added further mayhem to the gunfire in the arena.

It was at this point that I realized I'd not yet drawn up a will. It became clear that I would not survive the evening alive and I was chanting to myself, *huh, so this is how it ends...* when I remembered that the only thing in my favor was the fact that I was on top of a horse trained by Mark.

This meant that even with the Friesian stallion attacking us from behind and gunfire in front of us that things might turn out fine if I just acted like Mark. So, in spite of my chattering teeth and trembling bones, I did just that. And my horse reflected it. Albeit a little nervous, the horse kept himself composed. Someone swung open the arena gait, and we cantered in under huge spotlights in front of a crowd of a couple thousand people. We floated as if on air, as if my life hadn't just passed before me moments earlier.

Part of me thanked Mark for being such an exceptional horseman. The other part wanted to hunt him down on his date and tell him I would never again ride at an event with both gunfire and horses.

You do... What?

WONDERING ABOUT THE strange hours I keep and the dominatrix-like outfits I'm commonly spotted in at the grocery store, a new friend of mine recently inquired what exactly I did for a living. And it was in this moment that I realized how tricky it might be for an outsider to understand. My friend Karen held no fondness for animals or dirt, so trying to explain that my livelihood existed around these two things made for an interesting conversation.

"Well, I train horses." This, to me, seemed pretty straightforward until someone like Karen puzzles over something we in the biz like to overlook: aren't horses *a lot* bigger than us?… and stronger?... and quicker?

"You do...what?" she asked again. I could tell she was recalling fragments of *National Velvet* and any other anecdotal horse references from her past.

"I work with horses."

"And what exactly are you trying to get them to do?" she asked. To the average person like Karen, the sum of information about horses falls into two categories: what they've seen in Western movies or the latest Triple Crown race phenomenon.

At this point I explain to Karen that I train "dressage," which might be most closely compared to something like human figure skating or ballet in terms of how the horse performs. Then, I have to clarify about my analogy that, no, the horse does not wear a tutu or dance around to music. Dressage comes from a French word meaning "to gymnasticize" and teaches the horse to use his body a certain way and move his legs a certain way and…

"And they *want* to do this?" asked my friend, sounding suddenly like an animal rights advocate.

A legitimate question indeed. If I answered "no" it sure would cast a shady light on how I make my living. In fact, I could have cut this whole conversation short by initially answering the "what do you do for a living?" question by saying "I get horses to do things they wouldn't naturally do otherwise."

But of course we horse folks don't believe that. We like to think that our horses enjoy pleasing us and therefore enjoy their training. So, I told Karen that while horses may not dream excitedly of dressage at night in their stalls, they do like their training. But maybe more importantly, their owners (who keep me in business) derive large sums of satisfaction and...

"So, you actually make a *living* doing this?" asks Karen.

This is the part of the conversation where answers start eluding me. Admittedly, niche industries exist all over the globe. I've heard of people who make hefty incomes from inventing tools for social networking web sites. I know a woman in New York who weaves period costumes for historical Hollywood retrospectives. These are tiny little niches. But to the unacquainted, the horse industry can seem like the ultimae teeny tiny specialty. Karen was already giving me that "You *must* be a bank robber or prostitute; you can't really make a living working with horses" look I'd seen before.

But the second part of answering this question involved tackling the topic of whether or not I made a living. In the sense that I wasn't sleeping on the streets, then yes I made a living. But when compared to other potential income levels, a horse trainer's is comical.

"Well, no, not exactly. I mean, yes, I pay my rent and all that, but, well, no." Then, finally, I stop my stammering by making the broad pronouncement that "No, nobody in the horse industry actually makes any money, but...."

The confusion ensues. After a polite pause, Karen interrupts again. "If nobody makes any money, why do people do it?" Another legitimate question. Why, after all, would someone purposely seek out a tiny niche industry in which to labor tirelessly if not to make some real cash? Wasn't the promise of healthy incomes and individuality what drew people to niches in the first place?

I watched Karen's eyebrows furrow closer together as she scanned a patch of horse slobber/dirt on my shirtsleeve and waited for me to formulate a reply. But in my lifetime with horses, I have not found an answer that satisfies outsiders like my new friend. In the past, I've tried to explain that sometimes we do things because we just love them so much. It's the type of passion that sustains us even in the face of strained wallets. It's the type of passion that gets you out of bed in the morning and leaves you with that happily satisfied feeling at day's end. Didn't this make sense? I pleaded.

To the average non-horse owner, this *does* make sense. He or she has passions, too—things like European travel, family, food. But passions that involve wrangling really large beasts and being covered in dirt? Nope. How about doing this for minimal income? Double nope.

At this point, Karen had changed her confusion to a blank stare, as most people do at the same point in this conversation. And then I just shut up. I introspected briefly, stumbling upon the realization that *wow, I had a really strange job.* I'd definitely been blissfully ignorant of that before. Previously, it was *they* (the non-horse folks) who did not understand matters. Now, it became clear that the clueless one was *me.*

Yet, I couldn't say that I felt like running off and getting a "real" job in that moment. I intended to keep doing what I was doing, though with a new recognition of how odd it was. I pushed my chest out, held my chin high and found the answer to Karen's question about why people choose to be horse trainers.

I met her blank stare with a smile and replied, "We're all *freaks.* That's why."

A Little Bad Weather

Truthfully, I wanted to be offended but knew I couldn't. I didn't need a single moment of reflection to admit my student's husband was accurate when he cupped his hands around his mouth and shouted through the wind, "You guys are insane!" Then, he turned and climbed into a warm truck and drove away, promising to pick her up later.

We watched him drive down the road on his way to a cozy office as we stood in an arena that looked more like frozen tundra than a dressage court. The thought hadn't occurred to us earlier, but we now wondered if maybe we should have canceled our lesson. I mean, was frostbite worth all this? Moreover, what kind of instruction could take place in these elements? It seemed unlikely she would be able to hear most of my instruction through the swirling storm. And the freezing rain and hail falling on us made it tricky for her to see where she was riding.

She and I looked at each other briefly through the peepholes of our multi-layered waterproof thermals. Her puffy coats made her look like an astronaut. I, meanwhile, resembled a musher ready to tackle the Iditarod. We sniffled, sneezed, and wiped frozen tears from our cheeks. Then, through a series of silent gestures—a nod, a toe kicking the icy soil—we communicated to each other that of course we *would not* cancel the lesson. Without saying it aloud, we agreed, "We're *horse people*, for God's sake, now let's get on with this." You see, being 'horse people' means that both extreme weather and suffering are routine occurrences.

We horse folks regularly participate in activities during weather miserable enough to cancel ordinary events. Normal people postpone weddings or cancel reunions and graduations for torrential downpours, but we on the other hand still hold our horse shows, clinics, or group rides. Admittedly, we won't join friends for a hike in the rain or watch a ball game when it's freezing. But a horse event? Sure thing! When the weather turns so inclement we can barely see our hands in front of our faces, we hesitate only a nanosecond before saddling up.

It's almost as if we contracted for foul weather in our lives with horses, whereas elsewhere we have more sense. A lot more. I, for one, would never ride my bicycle in rain, hail, mud, or snow. However, I regularly ride horses in the same elements. In fact, I recently schooled a client's horse while chunks of hail bounced off my face and froze into the horse's mane. Following the episode, a friend questioned my sanity, to which I replied, "I'm a *horse person.*" Didn't that explain things?

A student of mine returned last week from a 50-mile endurance ride in the high Sierras and, except for 'a little bad weather,' she said the event went exceptionally well. Her Arabian gelding felt really strong and she had a lovely ride, finishing nearly in the top ten. Later, and only indirectly, did she mention anything more about the 'little bad weather' that obviously did not mar her experience. As spring days sometimes do in the Sierras, the weather changed mid-day from 75 degrees and sunny to freezing rain and snow. This happened in one hour, with riders 25 miles into the race. My student was perspiring in her halter top one moment and then scraping snow off her bare arms the next. Her horse's sweat froze to his rump and his muscles stiffened. Miraculously, neither of them got hypothermia.

If the average person were sent out on the back of a horse to gallop through a snowstorm wearing only a halter top, she'd be grumpy to say the least. In fact, she'd probably be venomous with dislike. And yet my student had nothing but an upbeat report of her time in the Sierras.

It's these encounters that leave me wondering *what is wrong with horse people*?

Perhaps we lack the ability to see miserable situations for what they really are. Or we pride ourselves on this defect. Thus, a teeth-gnashing ride over 5,000 foot peaks in a Sierra snowstorm becomes only "a little bad weather."

At least we do acknowledge that other people view us as not completely normal. In fact, this becomes a part of our identity that we're proudest of. We then take efforts to ensure we don't change this status and accidentally slip over to the normal column. So, we organize and participate in events that highlight our fondness for physical discomfort.

Back East, my family participated every spring in a competition called the Tunbridge Mud Ride, a 25-mile competitive trail event. In New England, competitive trail season typically runs from late June to September. However, this one event happened every year in March and promised all things miserable: temperatures ranging from plain cold to record-breaking cold, a poorly marked trail, crappy prizes, and mud. Lots and lots of mud. If the event had adopted a slogan, it might have been "Survive it if You Can." Nobody ever set out to *win* the competition. More or less, we all just wanted to test ourselves (and mounts) to complete something that didn't have one scrap of pleasure to it.

So, we awoke at 4:30am on a frigid March morning and embalmed ourselves in rain-proof gear and made it to the trail head for a 6am start. Near the start line, a few soggy donuts sat in a wilted cardboard box, the ride's only consolation for the 30 or so of us idiots that showed up. Then, the gun sounded, and we all galloped off into the mud. After the first couple years at the Mud Ride, we wised up to the trick of binding our horses' tails in big knots covered with about a half roll of duct tape. Otherwise, it could take a week to finally brush out the tight stalagmites of muck that accumulated over the four hour ride. With our ankle-length rain coats flapping and our horses' tail stubs wrapped in silver tape, we looked more like Bedouin-warriors-meet-New-England-weather than serious equestrian competitors.

Driven onward by a sugary high from the soggy donuts plus the nuisance of rain and mud flinging up in my face, I usually tried to finish the ride as swiftly as possible. But that mud thwarted me, ALL that mud. In some places on the trail, it rose over the horses' fetlocks and mid-way up their legs. They could do nothing more than stumble and flail through these sections, which slowed the pace to a crawl. Meanwhile, the motion of yanking their feet up out of the muck caused such a lurching motion that we all grabbed our saddle pommels and hunkered down like bull riders, our spines whipped around like reeds in the wind. Fortunately, the *suck, suck, suck* sound of hooves battling mud was hypnotic and lulled our minds away from 1.) the sugary donut buzz, 2.) our pulverized spinal columns, and 3.) the pounds of accumulated dirt in the corner of our eyes.

Once through these particularly heinous sections, I tried to pick up the speed again, although the quicker tempo meant increased punishment in the saddle. At speeds over 6 m.p.h., the rain needled against my face. After as much of this stabbing as I could handle, I averted my face to the ground, which meant I was abandoning all attempts to see the trail and to steer. Honestly, my spirits were so low by now, though, that I didn't really care if my horse ran straight off the trail and got disqualified. All I could think about was a warm bed.

Except for smacking my skull against some very low hanging tree branches, my mare always piloted us both to the finish line. Then, some helpers began the task of prying my frozen legs from her sides, an activity that sent daggers up my aching spine. But it was important to get into dry clothing so that hyperthermia didn't set in before the awards ceremony. One year, I managed to win my age category at the Mud Ride. Actually, I shouldn't say that *I* won it, but rather my horse won it since after mile #12, I stopped looking, steering, or even caring where we were going. *She* traversed the rest of the trail entirely on her own with me onboard grumbling that I would never again ride this stupid event.

Nonetheless, we won one of Tunbridge's crappy prizes. *Would a real trophy have been too much to ask for after enduring intolerable conditions for four hours?*, I pondered as I fought back the frostbite trying to creep up my ankles. Instead, I got a recycled paper tissue box with a plastic horse figurine glued atop. I guess it was meant to be funny in its own trashy way. It just made me even grumpier. But I had to admit that this was all part of the deal. All this nonsense somehow *did* make sense. We were *horse people*. And that explained it all.

Trendsetter

THE HORSE-HUMAN PARTNERSHIP struck me as especially remarkable last week as I slurped a fermented yeasty beverage at Whole Foods market. We humans are just so different from our equine friends. In fact, we lack most of the traits that we love about horses. Take simplicity, for one.

Being creatures of habit, horses are almost foolishly simple. For 20-plus years, they will get excited every day for their same bucket of grain or patch of green grass. They never stomp their feet and demand different flavors of grass or a more modern bucket. Nope, they just feel the same excitement for the same thing at the same time every day.

Then there's us humans, about whom the same thing cannot be said. Evidence to this fact: me slurping a fermented yeasty—and foul-tasting—beverage last week. This cup of bubbling Kombucha had made its way into my hands via some compelling marketing at Whole Foods. I had been drawn in by the fancy signage, the promises of better health, intelligence, strength, productivity, etc. Actually, the sign nearly promised that, upon consuming Kombucha, each customer would instantly become a rock star or a wealthy supermodel or something along these lines. So, I plunked down $4 and sipped and waited.

In one word, I'd describe Kombucha as unpleasant. It made my taste buds want to jump up and run out of my mouth. Within minutes, my stomach staged hostile protest, prompting me to scout out the nearest restroom. Meanwhile, the Kombucha's acidic aftertaste made my eyes water. You might wonder if, after this disagreeable Kombucha encounter, I have tried it since. This is exactly the point I want to make about human nature versus horse nature. Not only have I tried the yeasty drink again, I've committed to having it every day. Why? Because, simply, it's the latest trend in the health world, and if it does turn consumers into rock stars, I don't want to miss out! You might recall that last summer's big craze was goji berries. For $18 per pound, foodies could get a bag of red pellets from the Amazon rain forest that supposedly cured cancer, balanced moods, induced weight loss, etc. This year, the goji berry trend has been replaced by Kombucha. And I, being a fickle human, have joined its ranks.

That's what we humans do—we hop from trend to trend. We like the adventure, the newness. And our poor horses, those noble steeds that love the same old same old, often get dragged into this trend-hopping with us. While horses will live happily their entire lives eating the same grass and grain ration, we humans like to invent all kinds of new concoctions for them. A few years ago, garlic had become the latest trend in horse nutrition. Promoters said a few teaspoons of garlic daily would benefit horses in dozens of ways, like increasing circulation, warding off bugs, improving digestion. We humans responded by buying up tubs of garlic powder and feeding it religiously.

Then, research started to show that garlic actually wasn't very good for horses. It may cause inflammation and irritate their stomachs. Oops. We all threw away our tubs of garlic. We were ready for a new trend anyway, and scooped up all the latest aloe juices and probiotic to treat our horses' now ailing stomachs. The hot new item—stomach soothers—shot to the top of every equine shopping list. Articles ran in every major magazine about stomach soothers and their unparalleled affects on health. Most recently, though, there's been some debate on how to determine if these products actually work or not.

So, capitalizing on this budding doubt, equine food producers have tried to launch a new trend—fish oil. Many of us feel like feeding fish byproducts to horses is just inherently wrong somehow. But nevertheless, producers are gaining ground and these products are becoming a bona fide trend. After all, they promise enticing health benefits: strength, healthier digestion, circulation, etc. etc. Bags of grain infused with fish oil are showing up in barns. Folks are eagerly buying special Omega 3 supplements for their horses, wondering how these steeds ever stayed healthy before. How *did* they stay healthy before?

That's a simple one. They stayed healthy by consuming the only things they need and still get excited about every day—grass and grain. It's us humans, not them, who need these trend changes every couple years. Nothing excites us like believing we've discovered the secret to ever-lasting health. Our horse friends are happy without further discoveries. They're content with a diet that's worked for them for centuries. I can't say the same for myself. I'm hurrying out to Whole Foods to gag down my daily Kombucha and I need to rush before this trend gets replaced by a newer one!

The Kiss

I TEND TO THINK that all of us in the horse world are pretty similar even if we participate in different disciplines. Surely, we're birds of a feather and all that, regardless of the fact I ride English but you might ride Western, right?

Well, sometimes this rosy picture of unity crumbles apart as I realize that there are indeed vast differences that accompany individuals from other disciplines. Last week, I bumped into this realization yet again while schooling a dressage horse in an arena where a Western lesson took place. The Western rider and I stayed out of each other's way no problem. But I couldn't help being distracted by the trainer's instructions for cuing her horse. To be polite, they sounded far too simple.

You see, in the dressage world, giving your horse a cue to do something (which happens at minimum every half-second), requires nearly a Graduate degree in Physics. For instance, a dressage trainer would tell you to make your horse canter like this:

"Half-halt-on-your-outside-rein-and-then-step lightly-into-your-inside stirrup-and-lift-your-ribcage-on-that-side-and-now-deepen-your-outside-sitting bone-and-draw-your-hips-forward-and-count 1, 2, 1, 2-and- give-a-squeeze-with-outside-leg-at-2."

Whew. It's no wonder dressage riders carry around the stereotype of being too serious and slightly uptight. Constantly wrestling with that much data input and output would be enough to give someone an anxiety disorder. Interestingly, though, after a while we all get used to it. Until I observed the Western lesson, that is.

The Western trainer told her student to get her horse to pick up the canter by making a kissing noise. If you've ever hung around Western trainers, you'll notice quickly that they use a kissing sound for pretty much everything. Want your horse to step over a pole? Kiss to him. Want your horse to turn through a gait? Kiss. Pick up a right lead canter? Kiss. Left lead canter? Ditto.

Admittedly, when I first encountered this Kiss phenomenon a few years back, I struck an uppity high-brow dressage attitude. Where were the nuances of training and riding? I asked. How was a horse supposed to tell from one slurpy wet kiss whether he was supposed to a.) canter, b.) go backwards, or c.) get in a horse trailer? Where was the micro-managing and hair-splitting of signals that we dressage riders have perfected? Surely, no horse could rightly perform without this impressive library of cues such as when, where, and how often the rider should contract her right inner thigh. And yet there were all those Western horses doing all kinds of things with just the prompting of their riders' lips pressed together. Huh?

I won't hide that my uppity attitude towards this Western riding came from a big dose of envy. Yes, my belief that the plethora of dressage cues ranked superior to Western training came from the simple fact that I had tried the kiss and failed miserably.

Several years ago, I was helping my cowboy friend Mark compete some of his horses. I was doing very well with them except for one large problem: I couldn't make them canter. Despite my years and years of training and instruction all over the world, I could not make his horses canter even one stride. I used the most sophisticated signals that my butt and legs could muster and still nothing happened. Embarrassed, I asked Mark for help.

His horses only responded to a kiss, he explained. A what? Were we talking about training horses here? Mark got a good chuckle that I had never heard of such a thing and more so that I couldn't pull it off. A quick note: Mark's perception of New Englanders like me is that we are, in his words, "frosty." That's his polite way of saying we're tight-lipped and rigid. I prefer to think we're simply reserved and cautious, but Mark had his own ideas, thus dubbing me the "Ice Princess," which I guess for a dressage trainer is pretty suitable.

After demonstrating several rounds of an appropriate kiss, Mark told me to ride off on his handsome stallion and give it a try myself. Already deeply humbled that I, the well-heeled dressage trainer, was taking advice from someone with a Texas drawl in blue jeans, I was determined to nail this thing. I launched into a big ground-covering trot with his Arabian stallion, aimed for the corner where I wanted to canter, and then squeezed my lips together. And made a sound like spitting out a cherry pit. I tried again quickly and this time sounded like I was sucking food from my teeth. The horse kept trotting. I pursed, blew spit. We never cantered.

Mark told me if I were ever going to nail that kiss, I'd need to be a whole lot less "frosty." That meant, of course, I needed to act like less of a dressage rider. Like not sitting stone-faced with a broomstick stuck down my jacket. Like not trying to cue his horses with one-hundred fidgety nuances of cues at once. Just relax a little... and kiss. And don't kiss with that tight-lipped uptight look on your face, he said in his slow drawl. Maybe practice at home with a mirror like a teenager, he smirked, or read some romantic novels.

Of course, I'm reticent to admit this, but I did go home and practice. And I just never got any better than that sour cherry pit noise. I never managed any well-articulated slurpy sounds that even remotely resembled what I heard in Western arenas. Damn! Maybe what I previously thought was the world's easiest riding cue would be forever elusive to me. I, however, prefer to think that my tight-lipped failure at the kiss simply means I belong in a dressage saddle giving mind-boggling cues to my horses. So, nowadays whenever a Western trainer asks me to ride his or her horse, I politely decline because I'm still at home practicing that kiss with a mirror.

Are We Having Fun Yet?

Horse show season has arrived, which means riders nationwide are cultivating ulcers, emptying their savings accounts, and dreaming up stories to
explain the disappearance of these accounts to their husbands. All in the name
of fun.

Horse shows are perplexing things. Mostly, riders find them fun in some way,
which is why they choose to participate in the first place. But there are side effects
to showing that most riders either overlook or, in a masochistic way, also must
view as fun. These include 1.) nervously holding one's breath for days at a time 2.)
pacing in circles talking to oneself 3.) getting agitated by every judge, fellow competitor, and umbrella-toting spectator. Granted, riders each have different ways
of coping with these side effects. Some opt to chug a beer before they compete
to calm themselves down. Others let the effects of sleep deprivation render them
delirious and therefore less stressed. Everyone else just keeps insisting they are
NOT nervous, regardless of an anxiously twitching eye and shaking legs.

All the alleged fun aside, though, when you consider the sheer amount of
money and time that goes into showing horses, these events come with a hefty
dose of stress. In fact, if a person's job were to deplete her so much emotionally,
physically, and mentally, her employer would be under suit. Obviously, though, a
person is welcome to self-inflict the same stress in the form of a horse hobby.

As a trainer, I spend a lot of time at shows and I am always mesmerized by
the scene of women in the throes of exhaustion, fretting, and jitters. I see them
psyching themselves up to do something that upsets their stomachs almost to the
point of retching. Why do they put themselves through this? I wonder and then
watch as they give up time and money to wear an unflattering outfit to compete

in an event that will probably bring them neither fame nor fortune nor celebrity status in their communities.

For many folks with grueling home life or hectic work schedules, horse shows are the only mini-vacations they get during a year, which partially explains why people put themselves through it all. True, the event might bring some nerve-rattling moments and acid indigestion, but it's still better than the wailing baby at home or the never-ending errands list or the drudgery of one more day at the office. In light of all that, sleeping in a cheap hotel for a few days and riding one's horse in public seems dreamy. Thus, the popularity of horse shows.

But still, I've often wondered if riders ever re-think their eagerness to show once they've arrived. After they've signed in at the show office and found their horse's stall (that is flooded and appears to have an exposed electrical wire) and after realizing they've forgotten a lot of supplies at home (which will need to be purchased from the show vendor for roughly $300) and after their horse morphs into a bucking snorting dragon, do they ever pause to reevaluate their choice? At this point, do they ever consider that a two-day stint at a local spa would have been a lot less stressful and probably more affordable? If it's an escape from the hassles of everyday life they're after, wouldn't a cozy weekend by the ocean suffice better?

After many years of pondering, I think I've found the answer to such musings. I've concluded that riders suffer a type of amnesia that settles in approximately 10 days following a big competition. The timeline goes like this:

In the middle of a show, a rider will come to her senses briefly and realize that wearing a wool coat in 100-degree heat is somewhat miserable. Her head is fuzzy from lack of sleep and probably too much cheap wine at the show's 'welcome party' last night. Her horse's bucking antics in the warm-up arena this morning were actually terrifying rather than endearing. Her trainer is annoying her by pointing out things she already knows, like the fact she would have scored higher marks if her horse had not spooked and bolted for the gate during her dressage test. And in this moment of clarity, she vows never to show again. There just doesn't seem to be much point in it. She will go home, put this competition outfit in the closet for good and be done with all this stress.

Then, a week passes and her horse is back to his normal loveable self at home. In fact, he seems more gorgeous than ever. And, *voila*, just 10 days after the competition where she vowed never to show again, she has forgotten her frustrating performance, the heat exhaustion, and worrying how her thighs looked in white breeches. Totally forgotten. Next thing she knows, she's in her trainer's office signing up for the next show. And she's so excited about it that she cancels her previously planned weekend trip to the wine country with her husband for it. He, of course, does not suffer amnesia. Scratching his head, he'll ask, "But, honey, didn't you say you were never showing again?" He will remind her about a few low points from her recent show—things like the flat tire on the trailer, how the judge upset her with comments about her horse's "large head," and the fact she decided her trainer was incompetent.

She listens only partially, thinking what a killjoy her husband can be. Glancing up from the checkbook while ordering new show clothes, she replies.

"No, I never said that. Shows are really fun."

Move Over, Hank Williams

THIS MIGHT NEGATE any chance I have of being cool, but let me confess that I love Country music. It's a secret indulgence of mine, warming me from top to bottom and soothing me no matter if my mood is up or down. Plus, until lately I assumed it was synonymous with being an equestrian.

But I'm starting to realize—by becoming a very unpopular deejay at parties— that nobody else on the planet likes Country anymore, even horse people. This baffles me, because where I grew up, horse folks were the only ones who actually *did* like twangy music. The lyrics spoke directly to the simplicity and hardship of farm life. Nowadays, though, every horse person I know turns the dial when Randy Travis or Waylon Jennings comes on a radio. If cowboys of all people don't listen to Country, then who does? And what happened to the simplicity and hardship of farm life? You can't tell me Kelly Clarkson or Madonna sings about it.

I'm worried that Country is going to go the way of leg warmers and El Caminos.

Maybe the problem is that we've become too urban. Tunes about ridiculously simple things just don't pull any weight now. Who relates anymore to yodels about dogs or acoustics praising pick-up trucks? A whiney guitar and a ditty about old men sitting around talking about the weather just don't move people.

Fortunately for now, though, Country radio stations continue to exist. I can still hear Dolly Parton sing about her coat of many colors or Johnny Cash croon the Folsom Prison blues. For me, these melodies are a crucial ingredient in my life with horses. Much of this has to do with the hole-in-the-wall Country station in my off-the-beaten-path childhood town in Vermont. Back before things like automated programming or satellite radio, this tiny station—WCVR—ran from a four room clapboard shack, manned round the clock by deejays that were employable for no other capacity than what WCVR required of them: drink lots of stale coffee and burble into the microphone.

In the early days of getting our farm operating, my mother sold ads part-time for WCVR. Her colleagues included one drunk and one parolee. She sometimes brought us along with her and let us peruse the stacks of tunes while she hawked air time to livestock feed companies, lumber yards, and tractor dealerships. All these establishments, the backbone of any rural economy, piped WCVR into their shops.

This meant that anyone with livestock had a steady daily diet of Country music. No matter what errands you ran, you would hear Hank Williams, guaranteed. Then, if you happened to be a single guy, you'd inevitably develop a crush on the afternoon deejay, "Rena," and keep all your radios (truck, home, barn) tuned to WCVR so you didn't miss an instant of her sultry voice. Rena's smooth on-air persona defied her real-life stats. In person, she was neither smooth nor sultry. Rena was an exceptionally large woman, prone to sleeping in her clothes and forgetting to wash her hair. She told jokes without punch lines and then cackled and snorted at her own humor, sometimes stopping mid-joke to pop zits on her cheek. But if you only knew her on-air voice, you'd assume Rena was a real sex kitten. Thus the dozens of stalkers sending flowers to WCVR.

Then there was "Wild Willy," the deejay that took over from 6pm to midnight, and gave painstaking monologues about his latest heartaches. Wild Willy refused to play "new school" Country and held instead to a playlist of strictly "old school" music, though no one else knew what the difference was. Crooning, swaggering vocals all sounded the same to us.

We baled hay to Country, fed and trained horses to it. Like all farm families, our lives unfolded to a soundtrack of this music. But now, apparently, the horse world has shucked off some of the attributes that always made it less cool than normal society (things like overalls, chapped hands, maintenance-free haircuts—to name just a few).

Tunes about dogs and blue jeans and the weather have disappeared. It's not that they've been replaced by anything. It's more a matter of the horse world becoming more... well, maybe sophisticated is the right word. Nowadays, folks are busy with iPods and cell phones, email and digital cameras. There's no room for a twangy soundtrack in the background of one's life. Bruce Springsteen and U2 have ousted the out-of-date guitar pickers that Rena programmed daily. This all means we've become more modern and arguably more cool. Except for me, of course, because I've replaced WCVR with a station here in California at 95.5 on the FM dial that plays old school and new school, whatever that means.

Voluntarily Homeless

Iᴛ's ᴏꜰꜰɪᴄɪᴀʟʟʏ sᴘʀɪɴɢᴛɪᴍᴇ, which for many of us signals the start of good riding weather and competition season. For others, though, it marks an annual period of voluntary homelessness punctuated by events like sleeping in one's automobile, skipping showers, and eating whatever can be scavenged in a barn. I'm of course referring to the most selfless group in the horse industry: breeders.

During two months every spring, this segment of the population stops leading normal lives. Every moment is spent waiting for a new baby horse—slimy, delicate, and hopefully healthy. Any number of misfortunes can strike in those first few hours of life, a fact about which breeders hold their breath starting in February every year. Sleeping in their cars or the barn aisle begins soon afterwards. Skipping meals and all social interaction with fellow humans follows. Friendships are put on hold, household obligations suspended, national news ignored.

With the invention of birthing cameras a decade ago, many of us assumed breeders would now be able to lead normal lives year-round. The stall-mounted camera allowed them to observe their pregnant mares' movements 24 hours a day through a monitor in the comfort of their own homes. It allowed them to see the exact second at which she showed signs of labor and gave them ample time to put on their jackets and run out to the barn well before the mare lie down to begin birthing.

Somehow, though, these cameras weren't good enough. Breeders did in fact adopt the use of them, but still in the weeks leading up to a due date they continue to camp out in the barn aisle. It's almost like they don't *trust* these high tech cameras, as if the cameras might capture the wrong image or fog up at the critical moment, making a breeder five minutes late to a labor. That just won't do.

Instead, they rely on their old-fashioned sense of hauling a sleeping bag and a box of crackers to the barn and bedding down alongside their steeds amidst the dirt and dust.

I was reminded of this last week when an ordinarily reliable client of mine had failed to pay her bill for three weeks. Since this was unusual behavior for her, I called to see if maybe she fell ill or had a family emergency. She answered the phone gravelly voiced and sounding confused, as if her ringing telephone perplexed her. After gaining some bearings, she cleared her throat several times (most likely from hay chaff and sawdust) and apologized profusely. What day was it, anyway, she asked? Had the first of this month already passed?

Yes, about 20 days ago, I pointed out.

Oh. Well, was it still the month of April? Or did we somehow skip right over into May?

No, still April, I said. But well past time for a paycheck not only to me but probably other folks, too, like landlord, tax guy, etc.

Oh. Oh dear, she replied. She must have lost track of time, she explained, sounding slightly less confused now. Without hesitation, she told me she'd been sleeping on a hay bale outside her pregnant mare's stall, wearing more or less the same pair of sweats for weeks now. In fact, she couldn't remember the last time she'd spoken with a real human being besides her veterinarian.

The good news, though? Her mare gave birth to an adorable brown filly last night. And the little girl looked healthy so far. This meant that in another 24 hours, my client could probably comfortably move back into her house, start picking hay from her hair, and maybe eat something other than carrot chunks and oat cookies. Normal life could queue back up and my check would be in the mail pronto.

I chuckled to myself, knowing what "life as normal" consists of for horse breeders immediately following a new baby. It usually starts with the proud breeder referencing herself in the company of friends as a "grandma" and asking every one's opinion about potential names. I could picture my client at the supermarket querying the checkout clerk, "What do you think of the name Maestoso? Or should I save that one until I get a boy next year?"

The clerk, oblivious to what on earth she's talking about will stare back at her blankly, waiting for an explanation beyond the bits of hay stuck in her hair. Taking this as an opportunity to show off baby pictures, my client will quick-draw her digital camera from her hip and show the clerk a slideshow of a knobbly kneed creature teetering next to his four-legged mother. She will follow the picture show with descriptions of umbilical, colostrum, and nursing. The clerk, whose only familiarity with horses is from Hollywood movies, will wonder why this person doesn't fit her glamorous and coiffed impression of equestrians. Doesn't every equestrian in literature have steam-pressed shirts and shiny boots? And yet here is someone claiming to be a horse breeder clad in dirty sweatpants and a noticeably stinky shirt.

Other shoppers, too, will begin staring. Who is this curious person talking about newborns and flashing her camera to anyone within arm's reach? Due to the haze of sleep deprivation, a breeder at this point fails to notice that dozens of people are staring, curious about whether she owns a home without a working shower. These staring strangers are thinking the same thing I've pondered over the years.

Who would willingly exchange a warm bed for a scratchy hay bale?

Step-by-Step... Yeah, Right!

I'M NOT TRYING to shoot myself in the foot here, since I am after all someone who writes books about training horses. However, I flipped open a catalogue yesterday and was dumbfounded by the number of books, DVDs, manuals, workbooks, and other materials on the market allegedly to help people train their own horses and to ride better.

By page 40 of this catalogue with products promising results, I thought to myself that either horse people need things explained to them in a thousand different ways or we trainers have a compulsive desire to write books even though we agree that nobody learns anything about horses *from a book*. My mentor, for one, gets really feisty about this topic. He spews and sputters and paces around in circles waving his arms, trying to make horse owners realize they need to learn things from *their horses*, not from a book.

I tend to agree with him, especially since training horses is a never-ending learning process. Even after a lifetime with them, old masters still learn something new every day from their steeds. However, I also have observed how blissfully full of hope most amateur riders are. No matter the frustrations and setbacks, regardless of the financial sacrifice and marriage turmoil, their hope never dies. They have a will to improve their skills and master tricky riding techniques. And where there's a will, there's a way (and a book), right?

This optimism must be what keeps those horse book catalogues in business. Despite the fact that the last five years' worth of equestrian magazine subscriptions haven't given a rider one morsel of tangible, measurable, useful information about working with her specific horse, she will keep renewing. Never mind that the last dozen training books purchased at a recent equine trade show were so confusing that she never got around to reading them. And those instructional DVDs about how to be a better rider in four weeks? Those were both boring *and* confusing, so they're now collecting dust next to an old collection of Star Trek VHS tapes.

Yet the average horse owner still hopes that someday one of these books or DVDs or pod casts will give her just the information she's searching for. And that hour in the saddle every day will suddenly take on a new level of clarity and progress. So we trainers keep writing books and horse owners keep buying them.

We do have very good intentions in writing our books. We want to be useful and helpful and to give the average rider an "ah-hah!" moment. But the gritty truth is that each individual horse is so different in nature, ability, and behavior that no matter how good a respective book might be, its message will never be 100 percent applicable to *all* horses. Thus, Jane Doe the average horse owner buys the book on-line because it has a groovy title or at a trade show because its author gave an inspirational demo and goes to the barn intending to follow its instructions line by line.

After perhaps the first chapter, she is very confused and frustrated. She has followed all the steps so far in, say, "Finding Your Inner Dressage Path" but now it's becoming clear that her Mustang-Belgian cross actually doesn't care too much for the counter canter exercises called for in Chapter 2. And if she can't get through Chapter 2, does she just skip ahead to Chapter 3 or 4? Confused, she picks another training book off her shelf to cross-reference and hopefully find an answer to her puzzlement. But this other book suggests a lot of lateral bending, which her horse only does well in one direction. So, should she do those lateral exercises in that one direction and *then* attempt the counter canter in that same direction?

Even more confused, she consults her magazine subscriptions and finds an article that sums things up this way: if she sits perfectly straight with proper weight in her seat bones, her horse will execute a nicely balanced counter canter all day long.

Later that day, with two books and multiple magazine articles splayed out on the arena fence, she sits perfectly straight and yet her horse still turns into a chomping, agitated beast when asked for a counter canter.

Huh. Now what to do?

At this point, she might consult her friend, who will confide that she is in the same quandary. The friend may suggest a few other books to contribute to further confusion, or she may simply throw up her hands and admit that she's given up on books and other such information. But to admit this is nearly sacrilegious in the horse world. To admit that you're no longer buying and trying to navigate your way through manuals intending to guide you to the Holy Grail of horsemanship is akin to admitting that you're flunking yourself out of the community. Surely, no amateur horseman can find his or her way along without the step-by-step manuals that actually only work in an imaginary time and place where everything goes according to plan. Surely, stumbling along on one's own cannot be as productive as getting mired in confusing instructional texts, can it? Not in an industry with so much hope, that's for sure.

Stumbling along on one's one is just that—stumbling. Amateurs' vibrant hope, however, is an invigorating spark that lures horse owners into continuing to try things they've already tried and proven not to work. Just because all they've met with so far is frustration and confusion, it doesn't mean one more book or DVD won't cure this streak, right? On this note, I highly recommend that everyone purchase my second book that just came out last winter. I'm not kidding.

Re-defining "Fun"

NOT OFTEN PRONE to surfing the internet, I decided last week to buck that trend. I plunked myself down with morning coffee and logged on to a horse web site that offers 10-minute videos on every equine topic imaginable. Initially, I planned to check out videos about any discipline outside my daily world as a dressage trainer, like maybe an expose on spotted draft horses or the price of hay in Iowa. But then I saw a really curious title that yanked my attention: *The Fun of Dressage*. What? I read it a few times to make sure I saw it right. The FUN of Dressage?

Anyone who's spent five minutes either doing or watching the stiff-lipped sport of dressage knows that "fun" might not be the most accurate description. After all, we are talking about a pursuit based on trying to achieve perfection, not one where folks spend most of their saddle time laughing. I am by nature a studious creature, relishing in pursuits that require fierce concentration (which is a colorful way of saying I take myself too seriously), so dressage has always suited me. However, I DO recognize that we dressage riders quite often need a reminder to lighten up a little. Or a big "Chill Out, for God's Sake" sign hanging in the tack room.

When I stumbled upon this video, I thought maybe I found the golden secret we all needed. Perhaps this was something I could recommend to my students when they turn purple-faced from holding their breath and micro-analyzing the latest set of cues they picked up at a recent clinic with Mr. Famous European Trainer.

Click. I hit the play button, put my feet up, and readied myself for a good chuckle. Bring on The FUN of Dressage. Curiously, a stiff-lipped British fellow opened the first scene in customarily tight beige riding apparel. He donned a riding helmet and leather gloves-- everything clean and tidy. He stood in the middle of a perfectly groomed arena with manicured flowers landscaped around its edges. The camera zoomed in for a close-up as he reminded viewers that learning dressage can be fun. Just to give us all a sample of this process, he mounted up on a gleaming Warmblood whose trot looked so uncomfortable that it would probably bounce the kidneys out of any mere mortal who tried sitting it, except for this British chap.

By now, I became positively perplexed to see how this guy could transform the process of learning dressage from complicated/frustrating/fleeting to pure fun. I slurped my coffee and leaned forward closer to my computer screen. Bring on the FUN of Dressage, indeed!

The camera panned out now as this well-dressed British gentleman carried on in a bone-jarring sitting trot, trying at the same time to speak. Immediately his face flushed and beaded with sweat. His eyes narrowed as he described the correct riding position and the camera focused on his nicely straight spine sucking up the shock of sitting the trot on this 17-hand catapulting horse. His breathing became irregular while demonstrating how to hold one's legs close to the horse's sides while riding. Viewers quickly recognized that, were this fellow not in exceptional physical fitness, his limbs would be whipped around like a rag doll. He reminded viewers to hold their hands still when riding, and by now his face was truly contorted from fatigue and concentration. He asked his horse to walk so he could catch his breath.

So far, he hadn't said anything remotely humorous and he himself appeared to be in physical agony. What happened to the fun? I was still waiting for it. While regaining his breath, he gave the viewer a few allegedly light-hearted reminders. Make sure your horse uses his body properly at all times. Practice sitting trot without stirrups every week. Don't even think about going for a ride without doing a precise and consistent warm-up and cool-down.

And then the credits rolled. It was over. Surely, I missed something, even though I hadn't taken a bathroom break or even so much as averted my eyes once. Where was all the promised fun? For its alluring title, the video ended up being just like all the others in the universal Dressage collection. It left the viewer with that combination inspired/deflated feeling that she is pursuing a sport that is, well, very difficult. There's no way around it. Damn! So much for the golden secret, or at the very least, a good side-splitting laugh.

Ah well. I suppose I'll just keep my brow furrowed as usual and keep concentrating intensely. But don't worry, I'll let you know when I find myself having a really FUN time when sitting the trot without stirrups.

So Much for Harmony

WHO KNEW FENG Shui could be so unsettling? Here I was trying to add some harmony to my living space and all I'd met so far was disruption. Could this woman really be telling me to remove the horse photos and paintings from my walls? I understood that the sheer number of them might seem excessive to some people or that the fact I had only horse images and no humans throughout my house might appear anti-social. But did this woman really expect me to take down the pictures of pretty galloping horses with manes and tails sailing in the wind and replace them with photos of people sitting on a couch together?

She met my resistance head-on. Had I considered the fact I might have an obsession with horses? she asked. Well, duh, that's the nature of being involved with them, I blushed. Being sort of into horses is like being sort of pregnant. You're either full-on or you aren't. The way she said obsession, though, made me feel diagnosed. Like I had a problem, or something along the lines of an addiction that could be cured if only I would allow it.

To bolster my protests about removing my beloved horse paintings, I tried to explain the equestrian community to the Feng Shui expert. I steered clear of words like fanatical, devoted, and single-focused—lest I acquire more diagnoses from her—and attempted instead to convey us equestrians as exceptionally inspired about what we love.

I mean, it was perfectly normal for me to be wearing horse motif socks and a horse-patterned sweater and be drinking tea from my Thelwel Pony mug, I explained, because every other equestrian that came to mind would be doing the same thing at this moment. We all had horse towels and doormats, horse cutlery and Christmas ornaments, horse pajamas, horse key chains. When not at the barn, we read books and magazines about horses or watched movies like *Seabiscuit* or *Hidalgo* or Disney's *Spirit*. If all this were such a problem, wouldn't there be support groups or special therapists for us? To date, I have yet to see any listing for groups focused on "helping individuals recovering from horse addictions."

The Feng Shui woman, however, ignored me. She wanted to hang photos that showed me with my arms around family members, not childhood ponies. She wanted to frame images of me laughing and leaning into friends, not praising a sweaty stallion at a competition. She thought my office should have more candles and fewer horse show ribbons and medals. Ditto for the bedroom.

All in the name of harmony? Granted, I may have paid this woman to come to my house and share some of her expertise about the finer nuances of prosperity, harmony, and all that other good New Age stuff. But I now found myself in the odd position of pondering whether any of it was applicable to us horse folks. She could call us whatever she wanted. But obsessed or not, we with our cluttered homes seemed to have our own brand of harmony.

For an equestrian, prosperity means finding a good bale of hay for $1 less than normal. It's finding that perfectly colored saddle pad to match your horse, or having spare change in your pockets to buy him carrots. Harmony is the ability to sit his trot without bruising your bum. It's the compulsive desire to fill—and I do mean fill—your house with trinkets and images that remind you of all the special horses throughout your lifetime. Harmony is hearing your horse nicker when he hears your car tires arrive at the barn. It's the moment your trainer chooses the right words to push your skills without making you feel hopeless.

Yet, I couldn't find references to any of this sound knowledge in the Feng Shui materials. And the more I talked to this Shui expert, the more I started to think maybe we *were* nuts, we equestrians. Yikes. I babbled on and on about everyone I knew in the industry and how their passion for these four-legged creatures just doesn't get left at the barn. My friend Mark, who has trained horses seven days a week for over 40 years, still wants his phone to "whinny" when it rings. For his birthday, he wants to ride horses down a pretty trail (never mind that's exactly the thing he does 365 days a year).

Another friend of mine used to run home from the barn in order to watch horse videos on-line. Sale videos, Olympics, training videos, whatever-- so long as they showed horses doing exemplary things. My own mother, who has been around horses for what seems like all of eternity, still gets excited to decorate her Christmas tree with about one thousand horse ornaments every December. Then, she anxiously puts out her holidays horse motif chinaware, which differs only slightly from her everyday horse chinaware.

So, the more I talked to this Feng Shui consultant, the more I realized two things. First of all, she had never before dealt with equestrians. Secondly, she may have been right that we were a bit obsessed. But I wouldn't admit that part out loud. In the end, we struck a deal.

I hung some red cords around the knobs of exterior doors, said a few chants, promised to keep my bathroom door shut. But, if she so much as removed a single horse photo from my wall, I would break her fingers. Understood?

Murphy's Law

ANYONE WHO THINKS about owning a horse should know about an unspoken law that will eventually affect his or her sanity and check book. The abbreviated version goes like this: whenever something unthinkable and random can occur, it will. If you stick to this governing principle, you're all set. If on the other hand you neglect it, you're guaranteed some headaches and emotional turmoil.

Consider the following points as both illustration and warning.

- Even if you hire an electrical engineer to secure your pasture fencing, your horse *will* still find a section to break through during the middle of the night and end up on the neighbor's property. Costly repairs to the broken fence and horse's shoulder puncture are in order.
- Stabled in a stall with four padded rubber walls, your horse will find something on which to gash open his face. A vet will need to stitch the wound immediately.
- If your horse normally loads in the trailer quickly and easily, he or she will balk and refuse to do so on the one day you are scheduled to ride in an expensive clinic and are running late.
- Your horse will only be stricken with colic or other life-threatening illness when you are on vacation or otherwise out of town.
- After several months of having your farrier both return your phone calls and show up on time, he will revert to his former pattern of disappearing for long periods and not answering his phone.
- The trainer that you like and trust who you've been working with for years will decide to move across the country.

- Your horse will find a way to get his leg stuck in his hay feeder, no matter how high off the ground you place it.

This is just a short compilation to get new horse owners off on the right foot. After joining the ranks of ownership, you will add your own occurrences to the list. You'll find yourself getting used to unlikely and unexplainable happenings like they're standard fare. In fact, what we view as everyday reality in the horse world is so far-fetched that non-equestrian acquaintances think I lie compulsively.

For example, one of my students bought her dream horse two years ago. It passed the veterinary inspection with flying colors and my student happily wrote out a Cashier's check for the full $10,000. The next day when it arrived at her house, it stepped out of the trailer oddly and twisted its left front foot in the gravel. It has been lame ever since, no kidding. An uninitiated horse person would be bewildered at this point. She'd wonder *what are the chances* of such a freak accident? Her friends and husband alike would be bewildered. All of them together would stare into space and repeat *what are the chances? **What** are the chances?* But my student is well versed in the unspoken law that governs horse life. No stranger to the unlikely and unexplained, she took the event in stride. It's still her dream horse, after all. She just can't ride him.

I was on the other side of this equation last year, trying to sell a gelding that could have been someone else's dream horse. A gorgeous and friendly Andalusian gelding, "Fortunado" was super fun to ride and, had it not been for a bad run of financial luck, I would have kept him for myself. Instead, I needed to make a few bucks quickly, so I decided to sell him for a very reasonable price. Within four days of advertising on-line, I received calls from a bunch of interested buyers. It looked like I could make short work of finding Fortunado a new home and putting extra cash in my pocket! I hurried to the barn to give him a bath, clip his ears and prepare him to be someone's new dream horse.

The next day at 2pm, the first potential buyer came to see him. I got to the barn before her in order to attend to any last-minute grooming my horse might need to look his best. I, of course, wanted the buyer to be immediately smitten with him as if he were the most beautiful horse in America. I swung open the stall door to find the horse I had left in flawless condition the previous day now covered from head to toe in oozing hives. His skin looked like a topographic map with fuzzy edema pockets. His eyes drooped. One side of his neck was raw from scratching the hives against his metal feeder. I stood in the doorway speechless.

"Hello there…" I heard over my shoulder then turned to see the would-have-been buyer. She obviously did not fall in love with my horse. Instead, we called the vet and stood in the barn aisle staring into space together mumbling *what are the chances?*

With that particular horse, I discovered that the chances were pretty high. Over the next three weeks any time a potential buyer made an appointment, Fortunado broke out in hives from head to toe. His 'dream home' turned out to be a sanctuary in Northern California that promised to take care of these allergies.

After sending him off to his new home, I had a run of good luck. I didn't bump into the unspoken law of horse ownership for many months, so many in fact that I almost forgot about it.

A particularly feisty young mare that I'm training at the moment has been butting heads with me over our preparation for some upcoming competitions. As is often the case with mares, some days the training goes better than others. Sometimes, she cooperates willingly and other days she is pure devil. On devil days, I have a very tough time convincing her that MY way of doing things—and not HER way—is the best. It becomes a battle of wills and stamina. It turns into one alpha mare (me) trying to out-alpha the other. It has been this way for a few months. Some sessions go smoothly. Others go the opposite of smooth. All the while, I've been patiently guiding her towards these competitions, hoping like hell that the devil days get fewer and farther between.

And then a couple of weeks ago, aha! The ornery mare made a breakthrough. At last! For five days in a row, she performed beautifully. Her work ethic, her attention span, her willingness—everything was lovely. I started to visualize success at these competitions. After workouts, I brushed her lovingly and whispered "see, my way of doing things isn't so bad, huh?" We were becoming a little team, her and I. We were pretty darn ready to compete without suffering embarrassment. I let out a contented sigh. That was last Monday.

On Tuesday, I opened her stall door to discover the mare's right front leg looking like someone pummeled it with a baseball bat. A lump the size of a golf ball protruded from her cannon bone. I poked and prodded it. The mare lurched back and in those two steps, showed me that she was dreadfully, horribly lame. Yes, my young training project had blown a splint. Right out of nowhere. And now those competitions that, a few days earlier, had seemed so positively do-able looked like the farthest away things in the world.

The unspoken rule aside, I allowed myself a brief pity party. A feeling of unfairness hung over us. Here, this willful mare had finally turned a corner in her training and we were coming down the homestretch. Then overnight we got sidelined completely.

I mean, *what **were** the chances?*

The Unscheduled Dismount

INTERESTINGLY, THE AVERAGE riding lesson rarely delves into the skills necessary for a maneuver that faces nearly every equestrian at some point: the emergency dismount. Sometimes also called the unscheduled dismount, this rapid exit from a horse's back includes a moment of urgency, a little terror, and a brief heroic belief in one's superhuman capabilities. In a nutshell, it involves voluntarily flinging yourself off the back of your horse—most often at high speeds—onto the hard ground.

Personal preferences determine whether a rider opts to tuck and roll, land on her feet, or keep hold of the reins. After her first emergency dismount, a rider tends to bring her own individual style to the maneuver. A trademark, if you will. And from then on, this tumultuous parting of company from one's mount becomes a bragging right. It's a way of holding onto our human integrity, maintaining a sense of control. It's our mortal way of believing that, in the face of no possible good outcome, we made an optimal choice to rectify a bad scene. Yes, instead of going down with the ship, we bailed out early. And that therefore proves our intelligence.

Style aside, though, the emergency dismount is never a good thing. It's generally accompanied by life-ending reflections such as "*this* is how I'm going to die?" Nobody wants to imagine that her end will be met in such a banal fashion. And, let's face it—most riders really intend to *stay* mounted once they get astride every day. Who, after all, wouldn't prefer to be jogging around rhythmically *on top of* her horse rather than tucked into a tight ball flying through the air ready for impact with the ground?

For obvious reasons, the emergency dismount quickly ruins a perfectly good day. Not only does it physically bang you up but it bruises your ego, too. When your barn mates ask how your ride went, you hate to answer "Well, things didn't go quite as planned…" and then go on to divulge that your "ride" included jumping off your horse who you hated in that moment. In my lifetime around horse people, though, I've observed that after an initial few hours of feeling embarrassed and battered, riders use the mishap to explore the reaches of metaphor. Put simply, they start bragging. In fact, they end up embellishing the unscheduled dismount more than they do a perfectly flawless ride.

It starts innocently enough with the rider admitting to his or her coach that, after an unexplained something or other spooked her horse, she decided to bail off. Then later she tells the same story to her friend, except embellishes it with a colorful detail like this: "At first, I hit the ground running, but then I figured I'd tuck and roll, because why not? Well, after the roll, I was right back up on my feet."

Later that afternoon, she retells the story to a group of fellow riders, adding a little more flare: "After somersaulting through the air, I ended up on the other side of the arena fence, but I broad-jumped back into the arena, ran alongside my horse, grabbed his reins…"

By the time, the story reaches its final version, the rider performed a stunt that involved hitting the ground and then somersaulting *under* the horse's galloping hooves, then she sprung back up on her feet and swung her leg up and did a flying re-mount onto her horse. So, basically, she never dismounted in the first place. Not only is there less shame in this version of the day's happenings because it maintains the guise of control but it is so grossly exaggerated that her friends now view her riding abilities as far superior to theirs. When they in turn re-tell the story to their own friends, it takes on several more fictional anecdotes. By day's end, any truth in the story has been thoroughly lost.

All kinds of situations solicit an emergency dismount: young horses panicking in high winds, a violent spook, an accelerating runaway, etc. Just a few days ago, I had to perform a rapid dismount myself when I experienced equipment failure. I happened to be riding a nervous and high strung Thoroughbred at the time and had focused my full attention on keeping all four of the mare's feet on the ground. A fly swarmed around her ears and starting annoying her, at which point she shook her head a few times. The shaking must have loosened some buckles and before I noticed, her bridle flew off and landed in the sand five feet from where we were. It instantly occurred to me that *I was now on a nervous and high strung Thoroughbred with **no** bridle.* This called for an emergency dismount—NOW! Just as quickly as her bridle had hit the dirt, I vaulted off the mare's back. I collected the strewn bridle, put it on again, and got back to work.

Several of my students witnessed the episode and enjoyed a laugh on my behalf. But given that they *saw* my impromptu dismount, I couldn't spin any fanciful tales about it later because they would know I was just plain fabricating. As far as dismounts go, mine was pretty boring.

Admittedly, though, I *have* spun my own exaggerated stories in the past about emergency dismounts when nobody witnessed them. I've added a fictional somersault here and there, embellished the speeds of my running horse, etc. It's just so much better than saying *things got bad and I got terrified, so I jumped off.* This is why I know to believe only a fraction of what follows when a student starts out "Well, things didn't go quite as planned..." I've been in their shoes; I know how a few details added to the story can make the difference between sounding like a weenie versus sounding like a superhero.

All this rationale aside, I should get back to my point that basic riding instruction ought to cover the know-how for an emergency dismount because, like it or not, *every* student will be faced with one eventually. For this reason, I'd like to suggest that the American Riding Instructors' Association adopts the following operating procedures as required instruction for emergency dismounts. When a rider finds herself in a precarious situation on horseback, she shall:

Step 1.) Admit things are getting bad quickly,
Step 2.) Recognize that you are neither John Wayne, a circus trainer, nor a rodeo rider,
Step 3.) Say a Hail Mary and jump! Forget about gymnastic routines, cartwheels, or antics.

And lastly, simply admit to your trainer and fellow barn mates that you bailed off. Never mind any embellishment because, after reading this, they will know you're lying.

A Face Only a Father Can Love

SUMMER'S ARRIVAL MARKS a few things in the equine industry. Primarily, it indicates that another foaling season has come and gone, which means on one hand top breeders nationwide have created a fresh crop of future champions. On the other hand, it also means that hundreds of "backyard breeders" have new creations of their own.

Let's face it: we all know someone who has too much time on his or her hands and an old hay-bellied mare in the back field that he or she suddenly decides should have a baby, adding its offspring to the over-population of horses worldwide. Then this friend with questionable logic reads a couple of articles on equine reproduction and goes about finding a stallion with a cheap stud fee, no matter how good his genes may or may not be.

Twelve months later, the new "breeder" is standing back looking proudly at a poorly assembled and genuinely ugly baby horse then decides it is so exceptional that this breeding experiment *must* be undertaken again. This is where bad reason overrides finances, too, because the new "breeder" is usually incapable of supporting even one horse, never mind two or three.

The industry has a term for this kind of behavior. We call it "barn blindness." It is defined as the sheer inability to see one's own horses for what they actually are, especially the objectivity to admit that some horses are so mean, unattractive, or unhealthy that they should never procreate.

As a trainer, I like to keep abreast of the barn blindness condition by scanning the horse sale classifieds. Here, I find a breeder "proudly" offering for sale a Quarter Horse-donkey-Warmblood cross that more reputable breeders would consider only a genetic mistake.

I find promises of "highly talented" draft horse/Arabian mixes. I read captions to photos under a Neanderthal-looking head that say *gorgeous refined face*. Photographs posted by backyard breeders negate logic. As if entirely clueless about their horses' myriad of flaws, these breeders post pictures showing off crooked legs, splintered hooves, disproportionate hindquarters and heads.

Last week, I saw a photo of a youngster with a head measuring twice as long as his neck—a flaw so remarkable it defies nature. The breeder, however, captioned the picture with descriptions like "magnificent" and "special." That's the reality of barn blindness. Where *I* see a prehistoric looking profile that's barely recognized as that of a horse, the breeder sees a majestic representation of the Equine species.

After many years of providing me entertainment, the barn blindness epidemic recently struck close to home. My own father fell into the backyard breeding habit last year. A highly successful carriage driving trainer, my father also possesses the New England gene of stubbornness. This means that once he arrives at an opinion (after much hemming and hawing), he absolutely cannot be talked out of it. So, he reported his plan to breed his Hackney mare to a Friesian stallion.

Did you catch that? A *Hackney* bred to a *Friesian*. I immediately imagined the offspring—a prancing draft horse with skinny legs and huge feet. In other words, nothing any of us could be proud of. Plus, neither mare nor stallion had good temperaments or conformation and blending them together guaranteed a dismal outcome.

In his slow Vermont drawl, dad explained his logic, if I can call it that. You see, Rosemary (his evil mare) had been standing around the field for a few years and needed something to do, so why not motherhood? Plus, he had this testosterone-crazed Friesian stallion right here in his barn, he said. It all just made sense. So, voila, my father evolved from really great trainer to crummy breeder.

As a mother, Rosemary enjoyed the distinction of producing the world's least desirable offspring. When the baby arrived, it looked like something between a dinosaur and a Great Dane, dad reported reluctantly. He admitted that the backyard breeding habit may not have been a good idea. Regardless from which angle he viewed the foal, it was just plain ugly.

Within a few weeks, though, the epidemic struck. My father's own barn blindness developed and he stopped seeing the Hackney-Friesian for what it was. Suddenly, he started speaking fondly of it, planning a future for it, speaking of its "remarkable" looks and so on and so forth. He started referring to "hidden talents," the way a parent talks himself into agreeing to let his clumsy child try out for the gymnastics squad.

Then he said the defining phrase. "He's a pretty *neat* little horse." If I've learned anything about breeders, it's the fact that they use the word 'neat' when nothing else will work. In the absence of "athletic," "talented," "attractive," "competitive," a breeder is left with just plain *neat*. But what does *neat* say about a horse? Nothing really. I've pressed breeders in the past for more details and the conversation soon gets cyclical.

I'll ask what makes the foal so neat.

The breeder ponders this for a moment and then gives a puzzled reply, "Well, he's just pretty cool. I mean, well, you know—he's just a *neat* horse." And we're right where we began. When I ask if the youngster appears easily trainable or might be a future Olympic contender, the breeder again ponders briefly. And then offers a different version of the same answer: "Well, gosh, yeah. I mean he's such a *neat* little guy. He's going to make some lucky owner a real *neat* riding horse someday."

Call me a cynic, but I've known too many *neat* horses that have bucked off their riders, maimed their pasture mates, or just been huge disappointments to their owners. I prefer tangible descriptors like "strong" or "intelligent" or "well-behaved." If a horse can't be called by those terms, it generally ends up in those horse sale classified ads with a bad profile photo and a caption like "You won't regret buying this one-of-a-kind horse!" Let me offer my own professional opinion: steer clear of one-of-a-kind horses. They have been produced by folks like my dad who took a happily idle mare and turned her into the mother of the world's ugliest foal. I say let the mares stand around and eat grass. This will then result in a boost in gross national free time as hundreds of would-be breeders will no longer have to spend hours brainstorming ad copy for creative classifieds. It will also prevent the massive overuse of the word "neat."

En Vogue

ONE OF MY students arrived last week wearing breeches that defied the normally dismal fashions of English riding apparel so thoroughly that I went momentarily speechless. Not only were they electric eggplant colored but they had a five-inch tassel dangling from the rider's left butt cheek.

Stupidly, I asked if she *knew* she had a fringe swinging from her rear end. Of course she realized; it was a sought-after feature of this particular brand. Apparently, the manufacturer also made styles in various other show-stopping colors with tassels attached almost anywhere someone could imagine.

After moving past how bizarre I found them, I had to admit that I found the new brand of wild pants pretty cool and imagined myself in a pair of them with tassels swinging from my knees. And then, deflated, I admitted that I am probably too uptight to sport such fashions. It would be such a break from my stiff-upper-lip norm that I feared a total identity crisis. After all, dull-colored unflattering breeches have been a mainstay of my entire equestrian life.

A client of mine recently summed up how unfashionable English breeches are with perfection. She and her Western friends like to call our English breeches "dork pants." It's a pretty accurate description, I think. I mean, let's put it this way: I don't know a single person who reaches for her riding pants when she's looking for something really *cool* to wear. Now, if those breeches had tassels swinging from them, it just might be a different story.

For years, dressage riders have been begging to change the rules regarding competition dress code. How about another option besides white breeches and a black jacket? *Any* other colors, we begged. Hundreds, maybe thousands, of female competitors have lamented the sight of their thighs in tight white breeches over the years. Then finally, a few years ago, the higher powers of dressage announced new flexibility in the choice of riders' outfits. This news was met with cautious excitement. After decades of only white breeches in competition, what colors were now allowed?

The answer we got resembled the moment last week when I admitted that I probably couldn't fully break from the mold of dork pants. In addition to white, dressage riders could now also wear off-white and light grey. While this was indeed a change, I wouldn't call it a definite alteration of the norm. At the same time, dressage apparel manufacturers tried to appease us with a new fashion in breeches—ones with a high waist. Was it not bad enough to fret over one's cellulite in tight white breeches? Do we also need to pull them up to our necks? I pondered calling these manufacturers and explaining that we were *not* trying to look like our grandmothers and, to that end, we did *not* need our waist bands pulled over our boobs. What we wanted was cool style!

For so long, riders have starved for something about their outfits to be stylish. In fact, this is what ushered in the unfortunate years that I call The Ugly Pad Trend. About eight years ago, a saddle pad company caught on to a brilliant marketing reality: if it made really ugly products, people would buy them. And they would buy them for friends, too. In fact, people would buy so many saddle pads with pictures of frogs and zebras that the company couldn't keep pace with the demand. So, other companies jumped on the bandwagon and started selling their own versions of The Ugly Pad.

My own students showed up to their lessons with pads that glowed in the dark, zebra striped pads, leopard prints, coral reef patterns. At first, I tolerated these absurd and unflattering products because I knew how hungry English riders were for a change in style. But when the Fluorescent Ugly Pad came into my lesson, carried on the back of an otherwise attractive Arabian, I drew the line. Not only was this an atrocious color of pink, it gave me a headache to look at. Frankly, I didn't care that it glowed in the dark or that the rider paid $50 for it. I outlawed it.

To be fair, I also outlawed all the other ugly pads. My lessons now carried a caveat that I would turn away anyone without a plain old boring saddle pad. My students whined and pleaded but I'm glad I stuck to my guns. Other trainers that didn't follow my lead went on to pay the price.

The Ugly Pad revolution spawned an Ugly Leg Wrap and Helmet Cover trend that in turn ushered in ugly gloves and tack boxes. Trainers I once held in high respect were now teaching in arenas with gold glitter helmets bobbing up and down. Pairs of legs wound in zebra stripes trotted past. Students wore gloves with frog cartoon patterns and tiger prints. Things got pretty bad. It's not just that there were ridiculous patterns on everything. It's that every clashing color combination imaginable showed up. I'm no fashionista, but even I can tell that a pea green-magenta-sepia-yellow color combo is nothing short of awful. Or how about the plethora of orange and pink leg wraps I saw? We horse trainers have a hard enough time taking ourselves seriously and this bad fashion period made it downright impossible.

Fortunately, the Ugly phase finally passed. Riders came back to their senses. Either that, or a new generation that was *not* color blind came along. In any event, the world of English riding got back to its plain white and beige roots. Whew! I, for one, was back in my comfort zone.

Until last week.

Those tasseled eggplant colored breeches shook me out of it. I can't stop thinking about the sheer *coolness* of pants like those. As soon as I'm able to cast off my stiff-upper-lip personality, I intend to get a pair. Hopefully by then the manufacturer will not have printed neon frogs on them or decided to make them with a high waist. Goodbye beige dork pants; hello purple tassels on my buttocks.

Shorter, Smarter

At some point during the evolution of horses, Mother Nature decided to bequeath members of the Equine species maturing shorter than 15 hands an attitude suitable for global rulers, punk rock teenagers, criminals, or all three. Since then, every equestrian along the way has been humbled by a pony at least once.

Horseman's lore has long defined ponies as just plain ornery. But we trainers tend to dismiss sweeping generalizations like this. How can an entire segment of the equine population have orneriness coded in its genetics? Nah, it's just an old wives' tale, we trainers say. We then remind people that any horse's demeanor and attitude is the direct result of its handling and training. All those stories about ponies bucking their riders off and galloping back to the barn, or ponies that turn from angels to stubborn beasts back to angels in the blink of an eye—all these antics we trainers diagnose as simple training problems. Those particular sub-15 hand steeds have been allowed to do naughty things and therefore they continue to do so, we say.

Then along came Sally. Jet black, doe-eyed, and just 14 hands, this pot-bellied little Morgan mare strolled innocently into my training barn as a three-year old. She was the sweetest animal I'd laid eyes on. Or so I thought. She fixed me in her big-eyed gaze, sashayed her round rump around the stall and left me with the impression that I just scored a *really easy* training project. In hindsight, I can't stop laughing at this foolish thinking.

I would estimate that for 80 percent of the time, Sally is pure delight. She is sweet, docile, mostly uncomplicated. Then there's that erratic 20 percent of the time when she is devilish, sneaky, and highly unpredictable. And as much as it pains me to admit this, no amount of good consistent training will ever change these facts. If Sally were taller than 15 hands, I might stand a chance. But she never will be. So, therefore I am forever at Sally's merciless whims.

There was one particularly memorable afternoon at the Pebble Beach Dressage Show, a very high-pressured and classy competition, when 30 minutes before her scheduled class, Sally "colicked" in her stall. This is to say she buried herself in shavings, splayed out flat on her side, and could not be made to stand up. I got down in the dirt wearing my competition jacket and boots trying to roll her up onto her knees at least, but the little pony laid out stiff as a board. Panicked, I called the vet and cancelled our class. Within about 60 seconds of my canceling the class, Sally hopped onto her feet, shook off her shavings, and batted her eyes at me. Had she been *faking* sickness? Nah, said my inner trainer voice, horses *do not* fake things.

When Sally's self-burial in shavings began happening at every competition we went to, I had to concede that the blasted doe-eyed mare *was* in fact out-smarting me. She was faking sickness in order to get out of this stupid thing called Dressage that she was being made to do, she let me know. And the worse part? She is so adorable that it is impossible to hate her, even though you might try.

Sally sometimes goes months at a time behaving like the world's most perfect equine. She is so submissive and well-mannered that a complete novice could handle her no problem. And then one day, like today, half-way down the barn aisle she will stop dead in her tracks, grow roots, and refuse to move an inch further. She will become the world's most stubborn beast for a few sweaty moments as I cluck, pull, poke, and prod her forward to the cross-tie area to saddle her up. Finally, when she budges, Sally blinks those big lashes of hers and looks at me as if to say "What was the problem?"

Our ride goes no better, though. She spooks at an imaginary something-or-other in the brush, which sends her tiny body squirting straight ahead at light speed bucking and snorting. When she regains her composure (amidst much yelling from me), she again stops dead in her tracks, repeating her act of growing roots into the ground. I kick. I tap with the whip. I scowl. This is a horse that I have successfully competed all over California in all kinds of weather, noise, and disruption, sometimes competing in classes at 10pm, and yet here we are acting like she's never had a day of training in her life. She stands there flicking her ears, annoyed by my disturbance atop her back.

Finally, she obliges me and walks forward... and then swivels her neck around and grabs my stirrup in her mouth. Now we are cascading sideways towards the fence as a colleague of mine looks on in wonder. I know what she's thinking. *After four years in training, horses shouldn't do these sorts of things. But that's the thing—Sally's not a horse, she's a pony. The two are very different.*

Unfortunately, this colleague had also last week witnessed a mishap when I was leading Sally to turnout. I marched along in my ever-alert and attentive trainer's way with Sally close at my heels. Seeing my fellow trainer, I nodded my chin briefly to say good morning, and in that nanosecond my eyes shifted their gaze, Sally turned devil. Like lightning, she darted sideways, yanking my arm nearly off my body. Once she had me off balance, she kept pulling. Her target: a patch of sweet spring grass 20 feet away. I stumbled and staggered, trying to yank her back into my control. But I soon found myself ankle-deep in a mud puddle and looked around for the quickest way out before I ruined my new Ariat paddock boots. Damn!

Now splattering mud in all directions, I was still yanking and growling at Sally who had arrived at her destination and burrowed her face in grass (she avoided the mud puddle, by the way). "S-A-L-L-Y!!" I snarled as I tugged on her halter with a force that would dislodge a draft horse but not a pony, obviously. She again grew roots.

The other trainer abandoned any attempt at being polite. She now stared unabashedly at me. My face flushed with embarrassment. I knew how ridiculous the scene looked—me, *a trainer,* getting dragged around like a novice child.

In that moment, I swallowed my pride and all my former beliefs in training, horsemanship, horse behavior, etc. I heard myself saying out loud what I once believed was just a cop-out for explaining behaviors that hadn't been properly addressed. Trust me; I have addressed Sally's antics more than once.

"Ponies! They just do the darnedest things," I mumbled to my colleague. "I mean, they're just plain ornery, aren't they?"

Will Work for Free

A STUDENT ASKED ME last week what I would do after the quickly approaching date of my groom's college graduation and foray into the real world, leaving me on my own. I scoffed without giving it much thought. What a silly question. What did my student mean by it? I would be just fine after my groom's departure; I would handle things perfectly okay.

Later, though, I gave it some thought. With my groom moving away, I was now solely in charge of the daily operations of my business, the horses, and *myself.* Whoa. The last item in that lineup hit me hard. I jotted a quick mental list of my groom's duties and stopped after it exceeded several pages. Chief among her duties was keeping me in line. I now faced the grim reality of being a grown adult without a cheerful sidekick to clean up my mistakes, answer my calls at midnight, drive me around, and in some cases remind me to change my clothes.

You see, we horse trainers are fragile folks. We like to pretend that we are plenty tough, emotionally devoid, and self-sufficient. But in reality, we need a lot of ego-stroking. We are emotionally volatile and mostly, we get in our own way. We need someone to remind us what day it is, what our clients' phone numbers are, where the horse drugs are stored. Stuff like this. On occasion, we also need someone to point out that our eyes are bloodshot from too many cups of coffee or that we're getting crabby from not enough rest. Imagine the strain put upon a marriage to expect this of a spouse. Most of us are wise enough to realize the smarter bet is to hire someone who **needs** to be polite to us but doesn't have to share a home with us. Someone who won't complain when her duties include not only horse care, but also Christmas shopping for our mothers, cooking for us, picking up our dry cleaning, and washing our cars.

My own groom, the one who's abandoning me (er—I mean moving away to start her life), has more than once rescued me after my car broke down on back roads. She drove me to the dentist for emergency oral surgery one time and then waited all afternoon to take me home afterwards. She's picked me up at the airport at ungodly hours when I could find no bus, taxi, or train. After noting that I ate scrambled eggs for pretty much every meal, she taught me how to make Indian curry and tempura vegetables. When I suffered in bed through a major flu two years ago, she ran my business by herself for a couple weeks in addition to juggling a full course load at the college, attending to her ailing grandfather, and fostering kittens from the animal shelter.

Just writing all this down makes me wonder how I ever previously got by on my own. The short answer is that it really stunk. But I didn't know any better. I assumed grooms were a luxury reserved only for the highest paid trainers and were out of my league. Several years back, a fellow trainer enlightened me that grooms are **not** a luxury, they are a **necessity**.

My friend Mark, with whom I shared a barn for a few years, always had a groom around and after watching me exhaust myself by caring for—and training—fifteen horses alone every day, he recommended I follow his lead. Somewhat persnickety and possessing too much puritanical work ethic, I waved him off. I could do this all myself, I assured him, dragging my weary limbs home at the end of the day. Then, one morning I drove up to the barn and observed the scene in front of me as a hiccup of envy formed.

Mark strolled around the arena on a handsome Arabian stallion while a U2 CD blared, telling his groom in a single sentence to 1.) remember to wax his truck after washing it, 2.) answer his ringing cell phone, and 3.) switch the U2 CD with a Dave Mathews. The groom accomplished the orders within a blink, and happily. That's because the opportunity to work around horses and to get a foothold in the industry can be tough to come by. Therefore, young women line up enthusiastically, hoping for a chance to work for pittance in exchange for learning the ropes. They are energetic, responsible, and flawless. In sum, we don't deserve them.

I wised up to Mark's sense and got myself a groom. I've never looked back. Who else but some polite young woman who works for me, would put up with my ranting, my meltdowns, my pipe dreams? Who else would listen to my grandiose plans and not dispel them? Who else would shop for barn supplies because she recognizes my phobias for retail stores? And who else would possibly share a hotel room with me and never complain about my snoring?

Grooms are priceless, I tell you, truly priceless. I can only hope these young girls get the footholds they seek, because the industry will surely benefit from them. Meanwhile, I want to assure them that their efforts do not go unappreciated. Now, they may not be valued as much for the horse skills as they eagerly hope, but we trainers sure are thankful for their efforts in keeping us in line!

God Bless the Mares

MY SANITY AS a trainer had been called into question numerous times. The reason is because I love mares. Most trainers—perhaps possessing better judgment—prefer to work with geldings for the simple fact that they are easier to train. Much easier.

With mares, you get unpredictable moods, sometimes erratic work ethics, alpha issues, etc. Basically, you need to spend twice as much time to accomplish the same thing with a mare that you do with a gelding. But as lacking in reason as it is, the fact remains that I love them. I blame this affection for mares on my father. Put a bitchy mare in front of my dad and he goes all soft and mushy. He still denies it, but the content look in his eye when a mare is trying to kick him or bite his arm off is indisputable.

Worse, my father belongs to the small percentage of the horse world that lacks enough self-preservation to compete in Combined Driving Events. To the unacquainted, these events include hurling a horse and carriage through death-defying obstacles at the speed of sound. For these competitions, my father was well-known for always driving an ornery mare that no other trainer in his right mind would hitch to a carriage. And I had the misfortune of being hostage in the carriage as his groom and navigator.

At one competition in Gladstone, New Jersey, my dad galloped out of an obstacle, his mare kicking apart his carriage until pieces began to fall off. The crowd gasped. The mare squealed and charged, champing on the bit. My dad could be heard softly uttering "Adda girl, git up. Good girl." I think he may have actually been smiling as his carriage fell to pieces around him. I meanwhile wanted to be anywhere else on the planet except there in that carriage.

Somehow, he managed to finish the course in a record-setting time and win the competition. Afterwards, he sponged down his mare like a proud father. The rest of us wanted to kill her for any number of reasons: public humiliation, financial loss of broken harness and carriage, knowing the next competition would be a repeat of the same. My father, though, gently patted her and went to collect his blue ribbon.

The next event didn't go as well. We flew through a river crossing and up the bank on the other side when the mare repeated her kicking and squealing routine. This time, she severed the straps that attach carriage to horse. We were doomed. My dad, though, yelled for me to jump from my seat in the carriage onto the mare's back and then reach down and hold onto the shafts, essentially using my bare hands to re-attach horse to carriage. I saw this as the worst possible plan and realized my father's concern for my safety fell second to his intentions to win this event. Abandoning his orders, I decided to bail out before the ship went down.

Just as the carriage began to splinter apart around us, I threw myself out over the passenger side's wheel. In mid-air, I felt my dad's hand grab me by the scruff of the neck, interrupting my escape. He held me up with that hand while his other hand held the reins of his psychotic mare. His dramatic performance made the crowd go wild. The mare's back feet kicked within inches of my ears and my blood froze in my veins from terror, but I could hear my dad's admiring fans hollering and whistling. Again, he repeated his orders to me, this time through clenched teeth. And to help, he tossed me in the direction of the mare's rump, which I clung to with my best Spiderman impersonation.

I held my breath and fumbled under the mare's squealing belly for the appropriate straps. I grabbed whatever I could and held on for the remaining 500 yards. Miraculously, the finish line came before my death. Just as we crossed, every bit of our equipment fell apart from the mare's antics—harness, carriage, everything. I slid down to the ground and ran away before my dad came up with other brilliant ideas involving me and his kicking mare. Around me, the crowd went wild. Any other competitor would have safely withdrawn from the competition as soon as his equipment broke. But my dad risked everything and still beat the odds. Spectators love heroic displays like this and they thronged in around dad's beastly mare.

I was still within earshot when I heard my mother make her way through the congratulatory crowd. She elbowed dad's fans away and, after congratulating him on a finish line victory that would go down in history, demanded to know what on earth he was *thinking* sending their only daughter up onto the mare's bucking rump. He had no answer, already busy patting and sponging his mare. To this day, he's fuzzy answering what he was thinking that day. He insists that we all misinterpreted how dire the situation became and that he had full control of his precious mare the whole time. The rest of us recognize that his affection for that mare always clouded his perception. And now I'm afraid that's a genetic situation.

When I began training professionally, I soon realized that I was cursed with this same crooked affection for mares. The number of mares in my barn always counts double the number of geldings. At least, though, I have the sense to quit when there's equipment failure and I always have an explanation for why I like to work with these moody difficult beasts. I blame my father. Had he not grabbed me by the scruff of the neck that day, things might have turned out differently. I may not have learned to believe in the daring and the impossible.

Me and the Weirdo(s)

IN ORDER TO receive proper initiation into life with horses, it's best to find an off-kilter individual full of wisdom and wit to serve as mentor. Each of us along the way has had someone like this in our lives, someone who has nurtured our obsessive love of horses through encouragement and instruction. For me, it has been my mom. She has humbled me, humored me, and poured me a beer at the end of the day while reminding me not to take things too seriously.

My mom was particularly fond of putting her hand on my shoulder and telling me, "The fate of the world does not rest on the outcome of this horse show." She also taught me many concepts that will never show up in instructional horse manuals. I'll get to those in a second. But first let me explain that back in 1997, she wrote and published a somewhat esoteric book titled <u>Dressage in the Fourth Dimension</u>. To say she was ahead of her time would be like describing the Great Wall of China as a sort-of-long fence.

I read the book with a Thesaurus close at hand, a dictionary, an encyclopedia, and a large glass of wine. It was heavy stuff. In a nutshell, the book takes a metaphysical look at the animal-human relationship. Admittedly, metaphysics does not come up often in the context of half-halts and shoulder-ins, but as I'm trying to get across, my mother is not your ordinary horse gal. She paints, plays music, climbs mountains, kayaks rivers, teaches philosophy, and rides horses with the vigor of someone far younger than she.

Being raised by two horse trainers was undoubtedly the best childhood any kid could wish for. I never took a day for granted on that darling little farm of ours in rural Vermont. Alongside my parents, I broke horses, reassured horses, conditioned horses, and loved horses. And never once did I ever wish to be anywhere but out there in the country on that training farm. One of the many reasons I admire my mom so much is that she put me on a horse at three-and-a-half years old. The horse promptly shoved its head down in the grass, and I slid over her neck to the ground. But I've been astride ever since and I can't imagine life any other way.

Mom and I used to ride together a lot and, while I'm lucky to have survived this, it forged an unshakable bond between us. You see, my mother was incapable of simply riding a horse. What she did best was showboat. This is best described as transforming any mediocre horse that she happened to be riding into a show-stopper the second a crowd formed. Lucky for her, people stopped by our farm all the time, either wanting to walk around and pick raspberries or pet horses or just sit on the stone wall under our lilac tree. This delighted my mother. She immediately yanked a horse from its stall, jumped aboard, and gave the unsuspecting visitors a show they'd never forget.

Something strange happened in those moments when spectators clustered outside the arena door. Under my mom, a perfectly ordinary horse became charged with the desire to perform like an Olympic contender. Nags suddenly danced and pranced. Ill-tempered youngsters forgot their antics and went boldly through their movements with Mozart or Vivaldi blaring through the arena sound system. All the while, my mother appeared to be stoically schooling each one, rather than showing off for the crowd. But I knew better.

I remember these afternoons vividly because my own well-being was in peril if I chanced to be in the arena at the same time. One memorable day, a group of older ladies wearing festive hats walked up to the arena hoping to see a horse or two being ridden. Their timing coincided with my mother's favorite Bach fugue pumping through the speakers, which prompted her to perform a rather brilliant extended trot across the diagonal upon an Arabian that was normally lackluster. This delighted the six women gathered at the door; they gasped and whispered about the beauty of this display. Then, of course, my mother spurred her horse across several more extended trot diagonals and received more gasping. At this point, she was bounding around the arena at such volatile speeds that I could not keep out of her way. No matter where I steered my own horse, my mom came at me full-speed, oblivious to anything except those giddy ladies.

Finally, I just pulled my horse to a stop, figuring my mother could keep her showy display going around me. And within the blink of an eye, she rode *straight into me* at break-neck speed. She broadsided my mount so hard that we both undoubtedly suffered whiplash. My pony staggered sideways and I flew over the front of my saddle, clutching the kneecap that Mom had just nearly dislocated.

Undeterred, my mother struck up her extended trot, whispered for me to *get the heck out of the way*, and continued her show.

It was in that moment that I realized my mother was a little off kilter, but even though my leg throbbed, I couldn't help but idolize her. She imbibed passion, a rare spirit of leadership, and a remarkable knack for not caring when she slammed her horse into another rider. The cluster of ladies at the arena door swooned over my mother on that little Arabian.

Since then, we have ridden horses together all over Europe. We've gone in search of dressage in Vienna, Amsterdam, London, Lisbon, and Seville. Instead, we've found pig farms, drunkards, bad food, snow, and a few good horses along the way. We have laughed so hard that we forgot what was funny in the first place. We have disagreed, argued, tried to out-ride each other, leaned on each other, and been perplexed together. Horses have been the glue that holds us together through life's journeys. My mom used horses to teach me about patience, kindness, and what she calls the "spiritual economy" in the universe. Basically, live life with an open heart and life will give you back the same. This is the stuff in her book.

One day in Amsterdam, she put her feet up at the pub after our lesson, tipped back her chair and asked "Hey, did you see that hell-of-a-good extended trot of mine during our lesson?" I savor how her face is beaming, how delighted she is in her performance and whether or not a crowd of people noticed, too.

I'm sure someone *did* notice, but thankfully I did not. I have no broad-sided pony to show for it, no whiplash, and no dislocated knee. A good extended trot, indeed.

If I Only Had a Bran Mash

For the past two days, I've been so busy stuffing my face that I haven't left the house. You see, I just returned from a horse show and I've been in a feeding frenzy ever since. If you've ever been to a show, you'll know what I'm talking about. Either because of the time constraints or because there's nothing palatable around, people tend to just forgo eating for a few days or they shovel complete junk into themselves. They subsist at a frenzied pace fueled by French fries and coffee that's accumulated a film of horse hair by the time they get around to drinking it. It's a small miracle that they don't drop like flies.

After all these years, I still don't understand this. Horse competitions involve at least three or more days of grueling labor, sun exposure, often extreme weather, long hours, and performance. You might assume, therefore, that equestrians would feed themselves in the nutritional ways of a tri-athlete. Yet it's quite the opposite.

I fumed about this last weekend as I wandered the show grounds in a desperate search for something to eat that would quiet my violent hunger pangs. My options included; a sugary processed muffin from Costco being re-sold at the show's only food vendor, a sugary complimentary glazed donut and coffee tasting like jet fuel given out by show management, or a sugary baked good from the nearby Starbucks. So, basically, the only choice I had was in what form I wanted my sugar. I decided it was better to starve another day until I could get my hands on a piece of fruit or something without mass quantities of corn syrup. Now, just to be clear—it's not that I'm a health fanatic of some sort. It's just that I've learned my lesson.

In the past, I've succumbed to the "horse event diet" like everyone else. I realized rapidly that a growling stomach and light headedness was a better alternative.

Trying to be functional and athletic on a diet of sugar, corn syrup, and grease is like plowing a field on a tractor without a gas tank. After you get past the initial charge, followed by headache, indigestion, and crankiness in quick succession, you just fall apart.

Several years ago, a friend asked me to crew for her on a 100-mile endurance race. The 17-hour day involved setting up camp at designated spots along the trail to refuel her horse, check her equipment, administer electrolytes, etc. For those 17 hours, I consumed caffeine, corn syrup in a variety of forms, and grease of several types. By the twelfth hour, my insides felt like rats had been let loose. My head swam and my eyes throbbed. Thinking more caffeine might clear up things, I helped myself to another cream-curdled cup of coffee.

Within an hour, my internal workings crashed even harder. An achy fatigue overtook me and I decided the best option might be to sit down for a few minutes. Hours later, around midnight, I awoke to someone shaking my shoulder to see if I were conscious. I had fallen asleep curled up in the gravel outside an equipment shed and the dew had settled on me, which in a few more hours would turn to frost. The woman who shook me awake asked if I needed anything like a blanket or a ride home, but the only thing I could think to say I wanted was food—real food. Did anyone by chance have a hot sandwich?

What particularly amuses me was when I arrive at horse shows is the sight of people carefully administering bran mashes and electrolytes to their horses, ensuring their fine steeds will drink ample water and be nourished in inclement weather. Meanwhile, they themselves scarf down glazed donuts, ice cream sandwiches and whatever else makes them dizzy, red-faced, and worn-out in 100-degree heat. By the third day of competition, participants begin wilting en masse and I start dreaming about things like bananas and whole grain toast. The horses, on the other hand, fare just fine because they have been supplied with proper nutrition. Why their owners never think to treat themselves the same way baffles me.

Most likely, sometime around the mid-1990s, with a plethora of processed and imitation food products at their disposal, food vendors caught on to the sage capitalistic knowledge that horse show competitors are a captive market. Usually, the nearest supermarket is a 20-minute drive from any show grounds and competitors are tight on time. So, their one option for food is the on-site vendor. Much like in the case of movie theater prices, this has resulted in things like $3 bottles of water and $8 hamburgers. It has also resulted in offering items that marginally resemble real food but cost a lot more. After all, why prepare a fresh-made sandwich when a horse show competitor will shell out $7 for a corn dog nuked in the microwave for 30 seconds? Or how about some $5 cheese paste with those nachos? Never mind that the competitor will suffer digestive duress for the remainder of the afternoon.

Should fame or fortune ever befall me, I'd like to leave behind a humble legacy: a minor revolution in show vendor food. I'll call it the Egg Sandwich revolution. Years ago, horse competitions all over the East Coast always served up fried egg sandwiches. They included a buttered English muffin snuggling with two fried eggs and perfectly melted cheddar cheese. Nearly every competitor paired it with coffee and was then adequately fueled for the day ahead without sugar crashes or corn syrup highs. These breakfast sandwiches were always prepared hot by a grumpy old guy in a white aluminum trailer who traveled from one event to the next.

With one of his simple delicacies in your belly, you could tackle the stress of competition and inclement weather all day long and wake up bright eyed the next morning. More importantly, you'd have as much stamina as your horse that's been properly fueled on bran mashes and electrolytes. This makes a whole lot of sense to me. And best of all, it would eliminate the need to come home from horse shows and max out your credit card in order to satisfy a feeding frenzy like mine for the past two days. I've just about eaten my way through a grocery cart's worth of food and I'm nearly satisfied, so I better sign off now to find some place other than a patch of gravel to take a little nap.

Keeping up with the Joneses

I T'S NOT THAT a wild haircut or an armful of tattoos negates someone's competence to train a horse, but students tend to think that. I find this point paradoxi-
cal, since the horse world is populated primarily by free spirits. Nonetheless, when
a client seeks training, he or she is typically drawn to a professional that is, well,
clean-cut. Tidy. Smooth-talking.

Never mind that the most qualified trainer for the job might not fit that description at all. In fact, most trainers in this industry that I respect the highest for
their unparalleled skill occupy the margins of societal norms in terms of appear-
ances. Think odd fashions, social awkwardness, potentially offensive tattoos. And
then there's a population of trainers that have very little to no skill but present a
perfectly coiffed look. You know, shiny black boots and clean leather gloves and
steam pressed breeches. I once met a trainer here in California with the shiniest
boots I've ever seen, like fine black gemstones. But I don't think this person had
ever ridden a horse, let alone trained one. That seemed to matter little, though,
because he had the look just right. And that can get you pretty far.

I had this discussion last week with my colleague, a Western trainer, who wanted
to come watch one of my dressage competitions. She didn't think she could attend, she said, because the hot summer weather prevented her from wearing long
sleeved shirts to cover up her tattoos and she didn't want to offend anyone, or to
embarrass me. Let me clarify that she has more than a couple tattoos; in fact, she's
thoroughly inked from neckline to toenails. When first meeting her, it is admittedly difficult not to outright stare. During my first introduction, I found myself
obsessed with the question of why someone like her might want a five-inch swirling blade permanently colored onto her upper arm. I stared and pondered, stared

and pondered. However, I never once questioned her abilities as a horse trainer. From the first moment I watched her instruct a student, I knew this gal meant business. She focused like a brain surgeon and she elevated her students to a level of excellence they probably would never otherwise achieve.

Regarding her appearance at the dressage show, I tried convincing her that it would be just fine. Sure, she might stick out a little, but I didn't think anyone would be overtly appalled by her. That was the glitch, though. I didn't *think* anyone would be appalled. I couldn't guarantee it. Most trainers I knew—in any discipline—stuck with the same general appearance and mannerisms, and she was well outside that norm. But that's the funny thing. Everyone knows that horse trainers are an odd lot of folks. They're folks with unorthodox social graces, obtuse opinions, highly independent, a little rough around the edges. So, why then, do we all try to look the same? Who are they kidding with this tidy appearance?

Growing up, I knew a trainer around New England who specialized in breaking young, wild, or dangerous horses. Rick didn't work with good equine citizens; he only wanted the scary ones. Nobody could rival his skill with them. In 60 days, he consistently transformed unruly beasts into steadfast, reliable mounts. Yet, strangely, he lacked the number of clients his skills should have garnered for him. And that's because Rick was a bit—how to say this? —strange.

Every year in January, he traveled for two months to Florida for what he called "alligator wrestling season." We never confirmed if alligator wrestling is an official sport down South, much less if there's an organized season. But Rick went down there every year to tangle with the life-threatening reptiles and returned each spring with a few bruises and scrapes on his shoulders. He then spent the next eight months telling and re-telling tales of his heroics from those two months. Peoples' responses to him varied. Some bored of hearing the stories. Many thought he was making them up and wished he'd give up wearing his Indiana Jones style hat. Most, though, thought he was just plain odd, very odd. This tended to repel would-be clients, regardless of his skill with equines.

I pondered this last week—on the topic of competence, that is. Why would a person's appearance have any correlation to his or her competence? And how did we in the horse world make this tie? A former client of mine turned down my referral of a colleague due to the fact, she said, that she'd seen him wearing a t-shirt with large black letters pronouncing "BEEF: the non-vegetarian alternative." Would that somehow affect his ability to train her horse? I asked. She paused a long time trying to dissect the question. Then she replied that, yes, well she supposed the t-shirt made him seem unprofessional. In other words, he lacked the proper trappings of a horseman—leather gloves, collared shirt, pressed breeches.

In the end, my Western trainer friend with all the tattoos did not come to my dressage show. And, truthfully, I had to admit it was for the best. Setting aside my idealism, I conceded that she was right. Her lip tattoo really would stick out in that sea of women in designer wear and straw hats. And the five-inch swirling knife blade on her upper arm? It wouldn't only be curious to this crowd; it would be plain startling.

Nevertheless, my idealism still rears its head sometimes, like when I'm reading Dressage Today magazine. I'm convinced that one day, rather than the photos giving an impression that we all shop at the same store, we'll see pictures of horsemen of all colors and backgrounds. Just think about it. How cool would it be to compete for a dressage judge with a mohawk? Or how about one who alleges to wrestle alligators in the off season?

Of Strong Minded Women

S OME DAYS, THE mere act of surviving life with horses seems to mandate that a person forms tightly held beliefs about every daily minutia and to verbalize them assertively at any opportunity, lest you become confused or led astray by others' beliefs. And generally, a whole barn filled with boarders bumping into each others' fiery opinions guarantees an explosive environment.

I witnessed one of these impassioned exchanges recently while teaching at a new facility. During the middle of instructing my student to do a leg-yield, an array of escalating voices broke out in the barn aisle nearby. Apparently, one of the boarders discovered traces of alfalfa hay in her horse's stall after requesting that her horse *never* be fed alfalfa. The discovery prompted a meltdown with her shouting at the Hispanic stable worker who didn't understand a single word she yelled at him. The boarder then began hysterically combing through her horse's stall on hands and knees with bare fingers to remove any remaining blades of alfalfa. All the while she continued to scream in the direction of the barn office, threatening to move her horse to a different facility immediately unless the "incompetent management" at this barn could get its "stupid act together."

Her hysteria drew everyone around into a heated argument about whether she was being paranoid or if alfalfa did in fact present health concerns. One sympathizing boarder agreed that horses should never eat alfalfa and the hysterical woman's horse might colic from the offending scraps found in his stall.

Then another boarder quickly countered, "No, no, you're mistaken. Alfalfa maintains the correct calcium-phosphorous ratio in the gut. Grass hay doesn't. You have to feed alfalfa."

Someone else cut in, "Well, no, you're only partially right. It depends on the breed of horse. Stockier breeds risk becoming laminitic on alfalfa."

Yet another shot in with "No, all breeds can eat alfalfa. It's sugar ya wanna be careful about, but there ain't sugar in alfalfa so it's okay."

All told, the debate about alfalfa lasted 20 minutes, everyone offering well-researched and eloquent, albeit opposing, opinions. Absolutely nobody agreed nor was indifferent about the topic. Every single person in the barn held a firm opinion about alfalfa and, miraculously, none of them matched up.

The bickering about hay types segued straight into a debate about beet pulp. Again, a dozen fiery convictions flew. Beet pulp was good for digestion. Nah, beet pulp was indigestible. It should be purchased in shredded form and then soaked. No, the pelleted form was better and needed no soaking.

I withheld my own speculations about beet pulp, alfalfa, or any other feed because I knew in a matter of minutes, the conversation would switch to training methods, giving the group of arguing boarders another topic on which to weigh their opinions. And again, no two of them would share the same.

Students have complained to me in the past about this combative atmosphere, as if it's something that can change. They sound like they honestly believe in the existence of a boarding facility *without* clashing opinions and strong, feisty, opinionated women. And I have to be the needle in their balloon to explain why an opinion-free barn will never exist.

You see, numerous studies in the past decade have shown the majority demographic of our equine industry is women aged 38-50 years old. This alone explains argumentative barn cultures. Put simply, each of these women has already raised a family, led a career, and generally gotten along in life. She's used to having answers. She's used to being strong-minded and willful. Otherwise, she couldn't have raised a family or led a company or carved out a life for herself. Her feisty traits suit her well. Until she gets involved with horses, that is.

Around the age of 35 to 40, she will want to start riding horses again as she used to in her teenage years before Life intervened. She will start taking lessons at a local stable and then soon buy her own horse. At this point, she will find a facility to board her horse and join the ranks of other owners in that barn who annoy one another. And, yes, she will form her own opinions about the best brands of horse shampoo and leather products. She will decide entirely herself what kind of grain best suits her horse. Along the way, she will butt heads with other boarders that have differing opinions on the same matters.

These boarders will in turn label each other as "difficult" and "opinionated." As you can see, this is my point. The attributes of these individuals that have made them successful in their lives are exactly the ones that cause friction and "barn politics" in the horse world—willful, independent, strong-minded.

There's only one way to fix the situation.

We need to change the majority demographic of new equestrians. My premise goes like this: if women never had to take a break from horses between the ages of 18 and 40, they would not then be such different individuals upon returning to them. They would not be so accustomed to the firm opinions that family life, careers, and growing up demand of them. They would still possess the malleable open minds of their youth. So, to that thing called Life, I would like to say "STOP INTERVENING!" This way, riders could remain *consistently* involved with horses throughout their lives.

Trust me, if this became the case, barn politics would disappear. There also might never be a hysterical woman on her hands and knees trolling through the sawdust for alfalfa scraps. *Amen* for this.

Merry Christmas

SHOW ME SOME old-fashioned Christmas music and holiday ornaments and I'll show you an adult (me) who is instantly six years old again, filled with wonder and excitement and raw bubbling joy. Oh, and the belief that at exactly midnight on Christmas Eve every horse in our barn might speak out loud in a human-like voice.

My mom planted this idea in my head when I was very young, whispering it to me in the barn aisle while stooping low so nobody else—especially the horses—overheard this confidential fact. She shared it with such conviction that I assumed it might be an accepted truth amongst grown-ups. Naturally, I felt jealous that they had so many years over me of hearing their horses with real voices just like in the movies. So, I vowed on that chilly afternoon of Mom's revelation to do my best to catch up. Every year on Christmas Eve from then on, I would sleep in the barn waiting for my beloved four-legged friends to speak.

Nearly thirty years later, I'll admit that I have never once heard a horse speak out loud at midnight. It took only until I was ten to realize that Mom dreamed up the story as a way of getting me out of the house so that she and Dad could stuff stockings and set out gifts in secrecy. Her plan worked. I departed the house with my blankets at 9pm and didn't return until 3am, leaving them uninterrupted to play the role of Santa Claus.

Frostbite aside, I never regretted waiting in the cold barn as the horses chewed their hay. Year after year, I never felt any disappointment and I suspect Mom knew this would be the outcome when revealing her secret to me. You see, anyone who's spent time in a stable after nightfall knows the magic it embodies. When the doors are slid shut to the frost outside, the only sounds in that little haven are quiet, peaceful—horses munching hay, a rustle of shavings, barn cats skittering in the rafters. It is impossible, especially as a child, to sit in that space and not feel the magic of the animal kingdom.

After wrapping my blankets around me mummy-style, I sat on the barn aisle floor outside Equinox Black Silk's stall. Black Silk was my mom's cherished black stallion, a dramatic beast who acted like king of our farm. For hours, I sat cross-legged leaning against the front of his stall, waiting for him, Sunnybrook, Charlotte, and Trinket to speak out loud. Occasionally, he poked his coal black nose through the stall bars and rumpled my hair, warming my ears with his nostrils. Then, he went back to his hay to contemplate, I assumed, what he'd tell me at midnight.

Some years, I dozed off until the early hours of dawn, awakened by our barn cat trying to snuggle inside my blankets. Other years, I stayed awake by talking to the animals. Even if they weren't going to speak, they could listen to my musings. They could bend a compassionate ear to my worries that Santa's sleigh might get stuck in the snow or that Mom wouldn't like the slippers I made for her by hand from sheepskin and duct tape. The horses listened to it all—without saying a word in return.

Every year, as I walked back up the driveway, I pondered how delightful those creatures were. How peaceful and majestic. How much like the perfect best friend. A glance in our living room revealed that Santa had come and gone, without getting stuck in the snow, during my barn-sit. Several small packages peeked out from under the tree awaiting our little family to gather around in a few hours for a festive period of ribbon-tearing, sharing, and chatter before barn chores, snow shoveling and other duties called. How wonderful, I smiled on my way to bed, how divinely magical…

Whoa

NON-EQUESTRIANS NAIVELY ASSUME that "whoa" is one of the most important words in a rider's vocabulary. In reality, "whoa" has little significance in the horse world, having lost its directive power over the years of misuse. Nowadays, it gets used with the same lack of effectiveness as saying "calm down" to a child already in a full-blown temper tantrum. It's as if horse people say it just to see what *might* happen.

I've seen terrified veterinary assistants tethered to the end of a chain shank holding a snorting, leaping stallion uttering "whoa" incessantly in barely audible tones with blank stares and obviously zero conviction that "whoa" is actually going to *stop* the menacing beast from his antics. Likewise, I've seen owners trying to groom their antsy, dancing horses at a tie post, chasing the steeds around in circles with their brushes and muttering "whoa, whoa, whoa." Now, if they intended that word to actually mean something, they'd be darn sure to get a response when they said it, rather than continuing to chase their four-legged friends around to brush mud off their hocks.

I've lived a long time in the horse world and mostly what I've seen is that the word "whoa" is used with zero purpose other than to fill silent air and give our busy human minds something to work over and repeat incessantly. Here's a perfect example. We've all witnessed moments at a barn where something really awful is happening, like a horse starts panicking while in the trailer or rearing on wet slippery concrete. And how do their humans react? By screaming—and I do mean screaming—WHOA! at decibels that could rupture ear drums. Now why, I ask you, would a panicking and terrified animal suddenly calm down by being hollered at, especially by a word that he has been trained to ignore? Why would a whole bunch of yelling and shrieking settle the horse down? Well, obviously it doesn't. Yet, we horse people keep doing it. It proves that we have no intention that "whoa" is going to do anything, but it makes our frantic minds feel better. And that's what counts, right?

I've ridden frequently in Portugal over the past 10 years and the horses there are completely bombproof—except for Guinea hens. One year, the riding school's neighbor bought a flock of those clucking hens and housed them across the arena fence. When riding past that particular spot in the arena, our normally stalwart stallions bolted at the speed of light. It didn't matter how skilled a rider you were. The sheer speed alone ejected you from your seat and you could only hope to hang onto the stallion's mane until he ran out of oxygen. Of course, the flurry of bolting, charging stallions only excited the Guinea hens more, which elevated their clucking, which in turn accelerated our respective runaways.

Meanwhile, my dear trainer stood in the center of the arena quietly telling our group "Whoa. Whoa, ladies." He said it so unassumingly, as if it were our ideas to have a white-knuckled ride and we needed a reminder to rein things back in. Our cries for help, our cursing at the stallions and the hens—it all passed him by. Whoa.

Those years of Portuguese horses and clucking Guinea really confirmed for me how little punch the word "whoa" packs. So, you might say that like most riders, I had become programmed to say whoa only when I expected positively nothing to happen.

Then one night I was riding my buddy Mark's young stallion. I don't recall how the circumstances aligned for me to be in the dark arena at 9pm with about a dozen 4-H kids but there I was. The air was chilly, Mark's horse was frisky, and children on ponies darted around like air hockey pieces. I was just thinking to myself "This can't get any worse..." when the young stallion under me shook his head so vigorously that his bridle flew off. Now I sat holding reins attached to nothing. In its launch, the bridle flew towards the ground and the bit smacked my horse's knee hard, which startled him. So, he started running. I of course pulled on the reins out of habit, but the bridle was now dragging along in the sand next to me. Likely mystified by his sudden lack of restraint, the young horse kept running and 4-H children scattered.

I froze in the saddle, then quickly realized I'd need to be more proactive. "What should I DO?" I yelled over to Mark who casually watched the scene without concern. He gave me a look that confirmed I had asked the stupidest question in history. In his slow Texan drawl, he said "Well, tell him whoa."

I, in turn, thought this reply was the stupidest one in history. Why say "whoa" —a tactic proven NOT to stop a bolting stallion? Well, apparently, "whoa" actually means something in the Western world Mark hails from. Convinced that once again nothing would happen, I whispered "um...whoa?"

Upon hearing my feeble mutter, that young stallion screeched on the brakes so rapidly that I flew onto his neck, toppled over his shoulder, and landed on the ground beside him. He stood like a statue while I composed myself. So this is what WHOA looked like! The word *did* mean something! Granted, I've decided since then that "whoa" is like a Holy Grail and only precious few know its real identity.

Value Added

I LEFT THE POST office today after nearly filling the recycling bin with catalogues of nutritional products promising to make my horse sounder, healthier, more athletic, happier, and in some ways more talented. As I walked out into the late afternoon sun, I pondered how horses from days bygone seemed to live to a ripe old age just fine without all that stuff. No joint formulas or intestinal toners. No herbal mood remedies or hoof builders. At what point did we decide they needed scoopfuls of powders, potions, and pills, lest they not be suited to see the light of another day?

When I was growing up my parents maintained a 12-stall barn of performance horses. These were serious athletes, horses that competed only in rigorous sports like combined driving and long distance trail riding. And I don't remember a single one of them ever being unsound or having some malaise that left us standing around scratching our heads saying "gosh, if only there were a supplement we could add to his feed…." Our horses got three things every day: a pile of hay, a clean bucket of water, and a coffee can full of sweet feed laced with corn kernels and molasses.

But sometime around the mid-1990's, equine nutritional companies decided that modern horses weren't as functional as they seemed. Which is another way of saying they saw an opportunity to create a profitable market. In no time at all, they convinced horse owners that their steeds were compromised; they needed supplements. Thus began the burgeoning business of manufacturing products that promised to do everything from make a horse's coat shinier to settling his emotions. In fact, some supplements promise to do everything but clean a horse's stall for you.

Recently, a client of mine handed me a brochure for a supplement she had begun feeding her horse. The impressively glossy brochure promised the following for horses that ate it: improve digestion, create mental focus, tone muscles and ligaments, boost energy and stamina, reduce anxiety. That's an abbreviated synopsis of what the product promised. In fact, if I recall correctly, the yellowish powder was supposed to take care of every need your horse might have except for daily training. Maybe if you fed two scoops a day, it handled the training, too.

"What's in this?" I asked, noting that nowhere did the manufacturer list any ingredients.

"Who cares? Did you see what it does for your horse?" asked my client in a tone that indicated she might be thinking I was illiterate.

"Well, no, I'm not sure it DOES do those things for my horse, since I don't know what's in here," I pointed out. And, you see, this is why I'm often labeled a cynic. Before I plunk down $50 on a bucket full of granules promising my horse a better life, I want to know what's in there. What's more, I want some sales guy or gal to prove there's some real science behind the product. You know, like it's actually been tested and PROVEN to create the results it promises to. And by proven, I mean tested on more than one horse, one pony, and one donkey.

By this point, I was raining on my client's parade as she had been quite excited to discover this new product and I was obviously failing to take on the level of enthusiasm she had hoped for.

"Have you noticed any difference in your horse since you started feeding him this stuff?" I asked, trying to be upbeat.

"Well, no, not really. But it's just a matter of time," she smiled, conveying utter faith in the prophetic label on the supplement bucket.

"Uh-huh," I mumbled. "Well, was there any particular reason you started feeding it to him? Was something deficient or lacking in his health?"

No, she said. But things could always be better, right? Her horse had always been healthy and fit, but now with this new supplement, he would apparently be even better than healthy and fit.

"Let me ask you this," I said. "If I developed a fancy label and packaged Twinkies with this label promising that the contents would make you more focused, fitter, energetic and so on, would you automatically start supplementing yourself with Twinkies every day?"

After a moment, she understood my analogy. But that doesn't change the fact that equestrians hate logic. My client—like all of us—did not want the holes pointed out in her decision to purchase and start feeding this unproven magical supplement. At the end of the day, it made her feel good, regardless of whether it had any scientifically substantiated effect on her horse. It made her feel good to go out and buy something for him that was supposed to improve his life. And that's what counted. When she feels good, her horse feels good.

Dollars and Sense

A FEW MONTHS AGO, I found myself shopping for a new car. Apparently, this activity invites those around you to offer unsolicited advice. A student of mine halted in the middle of our lesson to try changing my mind about buying a new car. One moment she was trotting across the diagonal trying to get her horse on the bit and the next minute, she slammed on the brakes and delivered a monologue about my car search.

She told me I should instead purchase a used car because new ones lost value the second you drove them off the lot. She didn't want me to invest in something that depreciated within five minutes. With that, she finished trotting across the diagonal. My other lessons that afternoon followed a similar course. Far too many students advised me against "throwing money away" on a new car, albeit a low-end economy car.

I pondered all this unsolicited advice for a moment. Then, I came back to my senses and reminded myself that horse people operate with two different sets of financial rules. One set applies to their spending habits and life in general. The other applies to what they'll spend on their horses. There is a large disparity between these sets of rules. Take one of my students who advised me not to buy a new car as example. She flapped on and on about depreciation of automobiles but was meanwhile sitting in a brand new custom made saddle.

So, I asked what the difference was. Hadn't her saddle lost value since she first put it on her horse two months ago? It certainly didn't *gain* value the more it broke in. She looked at me puzzled. But how was her new saddle any different in depreciation than my potential new car? I asked. She didn't have a logical answer, which didn't surprise me. Her saddle purchase came from the set of financial rules applying to her horse spending, not from the set of rules applying to the rest of her life.

A bit of saddle depreciation here or there doesn't matter in the scheme of things. Where horses are concerned, owners refuse to cut corners. I once worked for a wealthy couple that used to spend heaps of money on special grain and vitamins for their horses but clipped coupons for $10 pizza on Friday nights for themselves. They also bought fancy stable blankets for their stallions and the most expensive saddles for each of their riding horses. A specially hired groom came every Tuesday with a collection of European shampoos to bathe the whole herd. But the couple meanwhile made a habit of wearing tattered sweaters from Goodwill and worn-out Keds. They looked so unkempt that most of their friends assumed they were dirt poor. Their multi-million dollar bank account was discernable only by observing the financial rules they applied to their horses.

Recently, a client of mine skipped a few haircuts and the dye job for her gray hair, which resulted in a frazzled, split-ended hairdo that wasn't flattering by any stretch of perception. She lamented how much older the bad hair situation made her appear. I suggested that maybe she should not have purchased a new snazzy curry comb for her gelding. Its absurdly high price tag could have easily covered a hair appointment for her. Plus, her grooming box already overflowed with every high tech brush, comb, rag, and curry ever invented. Certainly she did not need another. She looked at me as if I'd been abducted by aliens. Was I suggesting that *her horse* go without something just so *she* could spend money on herself?

My bad hair client is not alone .The oddity in spending habits among horse folks is so widespread that even those outside the industry know of its existence. A friend of mine who knows very little about horses pointed this out. I was reporting that so far the bad economy had not—thankfully—dented my teaching and training business too much. She stopped twirling her hair around her finger long enough to roll her eyes and say, "Yeah, but isn't it common knowledge that horse people will pretty much sleep in the gutter before they sacrifice what they spend on their horses?"

Sheesh, are we that bad? I wondered.

Within a second, I had answered my own question. I recalled a week earlier when I stopped at the health food store and didn't balk at purchasing several pounds of high-grade organic flax seeds (for my four-legged critters) but then opted to buy a pound of conventionally grown, rather than organic, bananas for myself in order to save something like 10 cents. I sort of knew there was no logic in spending more money on my horses' lunches than my own. But it just seemed like the right thing to do. Granted, it's still a long way from sleeping in the gutter. So far, anyway.

At the end of the day, we horse people probably justify the disparity the same way. Speaking for myself, anyway, I'd like to think that if things got bad enough, and long before I curled up in the gutter, one of my beloved horses would spare a little room in her stall and look upon me with gratitude for all the expenses I never complained about. This is what I tell myself when I'm writing all those checks. Oh, and shopping for that *used* car.

Alternative Universe

OUR LIFESTYLES HAVE adopted such a blurring pace that folks now outsource parts of their lives or just neglect them altogether. Horse owners are certainly not immune from this acceleration, but fortunately we have a remedy for these times where even reminders to comb our hair need to be written on a list, lest we forget. Unlike our non-equestrian counterparts, we can drive to the local feed and tack store for an injection of solace and simpler times where, within five minutes, our internal clocks will be recalibrated to a slower rhythm. I like to think of these little independently owned places as havens, so old-fashioned that they cause me an audible sigh.

The profundity of feed stores is that time stands still there. Just last week, I found myself fiddling with a multi-tiered chicken feeder one moment and then looking at squishy bottles to feed baby calves the next. Everything I fondled seemed devoid of any relevance to our modern times. It was grand! I inhaled deeply the old-fashioned smell combining oats, rubber footwear, and caged Angora rabbits in a nearby corner. I recollected moments with the exact same ingredients in various times and feed stores throughout my life, at 6 years old, 12, 15, in my 20s. Nothing ever changes in these places, nothing. Being inside a tack and feed store is so delightfully timeless and technologically deficient that a person can actually forget about cell phones, text messages, and day planners.

In fact, if a person were to spend an abundance of time in these wonderlands, her bonds with modern day reality would loosen pretty swiftly. Spending all that time surrounded by hand-held scythes, garden seeds, and livestock troughs can skew someone's perception of which century we're in. From inside a feed store, you might easily assume *everyone* led a homesteading lifestyle, driving their horse and buggy to market and raising hogs at home. You'd think that everyone in your mostly urban surroundings knew what to do with the oddities I played with last week: four types of chicken scratch, a sleek magnet for pulling nails from cows' bellies, bags of sodium chloride, seed potatoes.

It's definitely not your average retail browsing experience, though feed stores *are* predictable and that's what comforts me. Ironically like McDonald's and Starbucks, every feed store in every town across America is nearly identical except for small differences in floor plans. They all seem to have a senile old cat curled up by the cash register, a quirky fellow (or gal) behind the counter who has lived in the same town a lifetime and knows every scrap of historical lore. They all have stacks of free agricultural magazines by the front door and fly catchers hanging from the ceiling. There's a guy out back who divides his time between loading sacks of grain into patrons' trucks and flirting with women in the bird seed aisle. His sidekick divides his time between loading hay bales and napping. Some of the store aisles will be laden with cans of brass polish and leather dye so old and dust-covered now that they qualify as antiques. And no feed stores I know follow normal business practices like sales, promotions, or customer appreciation days. Nope, they all just keep marching along to their own never-changing beat.

The feed store of my youth—Braley's Feed in Randolph, Vermont—was a high point for me when Dad took me along on Thursday mornings. During my decade of visiting Braley's, the scene inside remained unchanged. Braley himself, grandson of the original founder, wore a long sleeve white thermal shirt under denim overalls no matter the season. He always lingered near the front of the store, flanked by four or five local farmers that came in every morning around 7am for the hot coffee and fresh glazed donuts that Braley set out between the Farmer's Almanac stacks and display rack of gardening gloves. Their conversation lasted the duration of a glazed donut apiece, or approximately enough time to comment on the weather, their hay crop, and the maple sap flow. Extra agenda items included the idiocy of members of the local select board.

Initially, I loved Braley's because of the glazed donuts. Then, over the years, I began to savor the *scene*. The brown braided rug by the front door occupied by a three-legged black Labrador, the way Braley wrote out receipts with pencil and paper even long after the invention of computers, the cluster of farmers or wanna-be farmers leaning against his counter with a cup of hot coffee and no other place in the world to be at that moment. The lazy conversation and Braley's opinion (he had one for *everything*) about the best type of salt minerals for livestock. The boxes of peeping fuzz balls in the spring that would grow into chickens by autumn. As I grew up and changed, Braley's remained the same, which in time endeared the place to me. It somehow made the store more precious and trustworthy to me in a world quickly becoming fleeting, changing, or deceptive. Braley's is in fact still operating in Randolph, Vermont in the same location, and probably with the same handwritten paper receipts, although it's a younger generation of Braley now writing them with pencil.

Last week, after spending more time than I realized in the feed store and pondering the purchase of nostalgic items I didn't really need like little cans of Bag Balm, I wandered slowly out to my car. A very busy day lurked ahead of me and, yes, I should have been moving at a frantic pace. Instead, though, I meandered. I clung to the slow rhythms of our local feed store here and thought about finding uses for a hand-held scythe. A noise startled me once I got back in my car. My cell phone rang from the passenger seat and due to my temporary time warp, I wondered aloud "What the *heck* is *that* thing?"

Greener Pastures

CALL ME AN idealist, but generally when I think of horses I simultaneously think of rolling green pastures in which to keep them. This is one of the reasons I'm often told I have a chip on my shoulder. You see, originally I'm from the East Coast, where pastures are as common as rodents. Almost any homeowner outside major metropolitan areas has at least one. With this much land, a person can happily accumulate horses to her heart's content and the horses will lead a happy grass-grazing life out there under the sky.

Here in California, it's another story entirely. In order to have a pasture, you would need to be a multi-multi-millionaire. In fact, in the town where I live, even if you were a multi-multi-millionaire, you would likely end up with only a quarter acre on the side of a steep cliff that will either disappear in the next mud slide or burn up in a major wildfire mid-summer. This is usually when I start saying things like; "Well, back East a quarter acre isn't considered enough land for a horse, anyway. Our pastures back there are at least 20 acres..." Most folks in California haven't owned 20 acres of raw land since the Gold Rush. And when I start sentences with "Well, back East..." people tend to roll their eyes. Frankly, they're sick of me talking about greener pastures.

So, recently I've been trying to stifle my comparisons about horse-keeping on both coasts and fully embrace my current surroundings. For instance, I've begun talking to myself when retrieving horses from stables the size of shoe boxes, saying things like "Yes, Jec, this is perfectly normal. Horses adapt to their living environments. Never mind this horses doesn't have enough space to comfortably lie down; he's just fine." I've become more at ease referring to a 12' x 16' area being defined as turnout where a horse can romp and kick up his heels. I've convinced myself that it is in fact possible for horses to be raised in sand lots without ever seeing or tasting a blade of fresh green grass. In fact, I've spent so much time trying to shed my previous paradigm about horse-keeping that some days I feel like I'm repeating a mantra in my new state: "This is normal. This is fine. This is just fine. Yes, normal."

Sometimes, however, I totally fail at convincing myself. Maybe this does equate to me having a chip on my shoulder, and so be it. At certain points during my day, I just can't help yearning for endless miles of open land for my horses and I to romp and roll in the dirt and relax. I can't help pining for the peace and quiet that comes from riding across 80 open acres without a sound except birds and breezes. Luckily, I'm able to snap out of these nostalgic longings quickly and get on with my day.

Last week, however, my mantra "This is just fine" suffered a prolonged blow. I was riding a client's horse at her property, which borders a *very* busy highway near our coastal town. Sometimes, the din of utility trucks, zooming sport scars, and Harley Davidson motorcycles can make it impossible to form a complete thought. I've often thought it might be more peaceful inside a food blender. Just to hold a normal conversation with my client, I am forced to yell at a level that actually hurts my neck. The horses, though, have adapted to highway life just fine and go about their workouts without being distracted at all by the nearby traffic mayhem. Truthfully, it's *me* that suffers more. So, I was repeating my mantra while putting this particular horse through his paces. And it was working.

Then a giant speeding SUV passed the arena and slowed down to watch us for a moment. The very second it slowed down, a ferocious bout of growling and barking erupted from its interior. The sheer volume startled me so much I dropped my reins. Confused, my horse trotted to the center of the arena awaiting a cue from me to do otherwise. I regained my composure enough to look over in the direction of the giant SUV in time to see an entire herd of Chihuahuas crawling out the driver's window snapping and yowling at me and the horse. Let me tell you, they may be tiny, but these little guys were out for blood.

Meanwhile, the driver tried to get them under control by rolling up his window which only agitated them more. They barked and scratched and yapped, all half dozen of them swarming around the driver, who obviously could no longer see enough to drive and was now blocking the road. Along came a Honda Civic pouncing up and down with rap music and piloted by a teenager in a beanie and hooded sweatshirt. The rollicking Civic slammed to a stop but continued to bounce up and down from the sheer volume of music pumping through its speakers. The teenager leaned on his horn. This, of course, startled the carload of Chihuahuas, spurring them into more mania.

It was right about then that my mantra completely failed. This was *not* normal or fine or even fun for that matter. Here I was trying to school this horse in the majestic and graceful maneuvers of dressage, all while under siege of yapping dogs and an angst-ridden teenager with a car that bounced like a basketball. No, this was not normal horse-keeping. Call me prejudice, but I'll trade the carload of barking dogs for a silent arena any day.

Horseplay

My friend Carmen's adorable daughter Simone is, against all logic, horse-obsessed. I, too, suffered horse obsession as a child, but unlike Simone I lived on a farm so my craze seemed mostly normal. Simone, however, lives in a condominium in a high-density neighborhood in a populated metropolitan area. Neither her parents nor friends share her equine enthusiasm; it developed in her apparently out of the blue. This charming little blond-haired girl now has horse pajamas, pony coloring books, Breyer models, a wooden stable, horse-themed Valentine's cards and cookie cutters. She is afflicted so severely that all the non-horse people around her can only scratch their heads.

To me, Simone proves a hypothesis from my trainer in Portugal. He said to me one day, "It's either in your blood or it's not." He meant it didn't matter what any person's financial situation, environmental influences, or anything else happened to be. If horses were in your blood, you were fated to have an undying affection for them. Some folks might not actualize this fate until later in life, he pondered, while others seize on it immediately at birth. Simone appears to fall into the latter category, which warms my heart because I did too.

As a young child on our farm surrounded by horses all day, I still wanted to play horse games at night, read horse books, or make horse drawings. I couldn't get enough. My elementary school teachers telephoned my parents on several occasions to express concern over my potential neurosis. Meanwhile, I submitted book reports about *The Black Stallion*, science projects about veterinary topics, history essays about ancient breeds, and I invented four-legged games at recess. My teachers panicked about this single-mindedness and told my parents to make some kind of intervention. As if they hadn't tried.

Indeed, they gave me Barbie dolls, bicycles, mini baking sets, and Lincoln Logs. But I only wanted horses, horses, and more horses. My parents had to give up and pray that I matured—magically somehow—into a well-rounded adult. And mostly I have. Or at least I trick myself into believing that. Then, moments like one last week rattle me out of that comfy daydream. I was chatting with Carmen on her couch when suddenly I noticed across the room a small stable filled with Breyer horse models. Childlike, I bolted off the couch mid-sentence (I believe we were discussing grown-up stuff like politics) and ran over to it. Simone joined my side instantly and I begged her to show me the little stable.

She obliged but only after her tiny hands showed me her favorite member of the barn, a thick-necked plastic draft horse. My favorite was the Appaloosa with splotches painted on his rump, although Simone didn't get around to asking me which one I liked best. She was excitedly relaying the details of her pretend farm to me, like the fact that all twelve of her horses were stallions. And the Palomino one didn't get along with the others. And that her horses had just gone into the stable for the night before I came over. "Uh-huh, uh-huh," I followed along, instantly a four- year- old again myself. Oooooh, my chest filled up with joy when I remembered my own Breyer stable and teeny tiny pasture fences and the endless hours of playing horse. I was starting to feel like Simone and I were birds of a feather, never mind the nearly thirty years between us.

Then she offered to show me the rocking horse that she'd received for Christmas, which I agreed to in a heartbeat. We skittered upstairs to her bedroom and within a moment, I gave thanks for the nearly 30 years between us. A lot has changed between the days of making up four-legged galloping games at recess and today. Namely, technology has intervened. Had I owned a rocking horse of the likes that Simone now possessed, I never would have stood a chance at being a well-rounded adult. In fact, I'm pretty sure I never would have left my bedroom.

Simone's toy horse is frighteningly lifelike. Rosebud stands as tall as a Shetland pony, is able to swish her tail and move her head and neck. She even chomps carrots and makes chewing noises. She is able to carry a grown adult on her back and when the rider swings her arm overhead and says gid-dyup, the horse actually does. Its body starts herky jerking and the fuzzy little technological beast makes clomp-clomp noises. When I pulled on the reins, it stopped.

Whoa.

Wide-eyed, deeply envious, and truly speechless, I curried this almost-real horse's hair and assured Simone she was the luckiest girl on the planet. As for whether she stands a chance of ever out-growing her horse-obsession, I'd say there's no way. But I secretly hope she does because I've got a place in my house already picked out for Rosebud.

Greener Pastures, Part II

I VISITED MY HOMETOWN in Vermont last week and was immediately reminded that traveling to the Northeast from California means boarding a plane in flip-flops and shorts and then six hours later trying to stuff myself into five sweaters at once. By the time I left the arrival terminal, I was wearing everything I packed in my suitcase. And I was wishing for one more scarf to cover the drafty parts on my neck not yet fully mummified.

My father, meanwhile, pointed out that it was a lovely Autumn day with balmy temperatures well into the 40's. I begged him to roll up his window and stop trying to tell me that the biting air outside was warm by any one's definition. It has been only six years since I left Vermont for California, but apparently one can soften up quickly. I used to laugh at Californians during January wearing their Ugg boots and woolen scarves as if it were actually winter outside rather than a mid-60 degree day with light breezes. But now I have become one of them. I wrap scarves around myself as soon as the temperature dips below the high 60's, I use the word storm to describe a light rain shower, and I talk about winter as if it's actually a season here (which it isn't).

While visiting Vermont, I realized just how soft I've become. Back when I lived in New England, I often taught riding lessons until I was frozen solid. Then I would call it a day, rubbing icicles out of my eyelashes. One year, I got frostbite in all ten toes and instated a policy that from then on, I would teach only in temperatures above 10 degrees Fahrenheit. The following year, though, I got frostbite in all ten fingers, and I raised the temperature minimum to 20 degrees. However, a horse trainer in Vermont cannot survive with such a policy as I soon found out. You see, during the months of January and February the temperature sometimes sits below

20 degrees for weeks at a time. This meant my prospective income-earning days reduced from 30 per month to zero. Thus, I moved to California.

Last week's visit home coincided with my birthday, and so my friend Sarah took me to her favorite tack and saddle shop. The idea was to buy me a gift. Not being a great shopper, I asked Sarah to help me choose a pair of riding pants. Next thing I know, she's holding up something that looks like a uniform for ski patrol in Alaska.

"What about these?" she asked, obviously pleased with whatever it was that she found.

"Um... well what are those, exactly?" I asked as politely as possible.

Her brow pushed together. She looked at me like a stranger, or someone who had gravely disappointed her.

"What? You don't remember these?" she finally mumbled, looking off into space now. I could sense an odd tension in the room, as if she'd asked me if I remembered my own father's name. I tried to ease the growing alienation I sensed between us. Clearly, I should have recognized whatever she held in her hands. And honestly, to me, it looked like a cross between a bathrobe and a sleeping bag.

"Fleece riding pants? Don't you remember? Do people in California not wear these?" asked Sarah, trying to fathom how anyone could survive in winter without insulating herself in four inches of unflattering fabrics.

Upon closer inspection, and a very chilly recollection of my former life, I did remember the fleece riding pants. I remember owning an entire drawer of them. They were thick and fuzzy and added at least three inches of bulk to each thigh. Well, I should say they *would have* added three inches of bulk if worn alone. But a rider would perish in Vermont's winter trying to wear only fleece pants. One also needed 1.) silk long underwear 2.) thermal undergarments 3.) heated socks and 4.) an external waterproof shell of some sort. In that order. All told, when I got dressed to ride in Vermont, I inflated from a size five to a size 10.

With so many layers of clothes, it's almost impossible to ride a horse. I mean, you are so padded and insulated that you can barely move, let alone feel anything like a horse moving under you. Giving lessons always highlighted this challenge. Riders would ask me about their form, their position in the saddle, etc. "Is my leg in the right place?" they would ask. "Is my back straight?" And I would stand in the middle of the arena staring at them, trying to see them through all those layers. Sometimes, I had to admit, "You know, I can't even see your back." A person could be entirely slouched over or slumped down taking a nap in the saddle, and I would never be able to tell under all the jackets and flannel.

But the beauty of life in the Northeast is that riders there assume that equestrians across the country suffer through the same winter experiences. They think the sunny portrayals of California are just a fabrication of Hollywood. Shivering with their frostbitten fingers frozen around a pair of reins, they believe we Californians are donning fleece riding pants and sniffling through riding lessons, too. Not so, dear New Englanders! I will always remain a Vermont native at heart and I do harbor a fierce pride in that frigid northeastern United States. But I have to admit that I don't miss fleece riding pants, no matter how sexy this year's color selection might be. I'll stick to riding in shirt sleeves and everyday breeches.

For now, I need to get going. Tomorrow is forecast for light rain showers and I need to go prepare the barn for this storm.

Hold that Smile!

I̲t̲'s̲ ̲n̲o̲t̲ ̲t̲h̲a̲t̲ I wasn't *trying* to be more serious. It's just that I found it very difficult at that moment given my circumstances. Let me clarify that I was competing in a dressage event aboard a Haflinger pony, which is akin to arriving at a Champ car race with a Nissan Sentra. Or showing up at a figure skating competition on roller skates. Don't misunderstand me—I *wanted* to look as pinched and uppity as everyone else in the warm-up arena. But, truthfully, I was finding it impossible to take things very seriously.

This threw me off because I have for many years observed the four golden principles of competing horses. Those principles dictate a competitor's behaviors in the following order.

Upon arriving at a show, a competitor shall:

1.) get nervous, causing horse to be excitable and jumpy;
2.) blame everything not quite right (including weather) on groom, spouse, or show management;
3.) transform features of face into constipated-looking frown;
4.) view the outcome of this competition with a level of importance reserved for World Wars and global warming.

Anyway, there I was in the warm-up arena preparing my mount for his first dressage test of the day and not adhering to any of the above principles. After dodging two erratic riders wildly out of control (and completely unaware) who would have otherwise smashed into me, I reminded myself to sit up and assume the "dressage position." This would help me align with step #3 above and thereby blend in with everyone around me. I screwed my face into a stern frown, sat ram-rod stiff, and conducted myself with an air of utter importance.

But within a moment, I realized I wasn't kidding anyone, especially myself. The fact still remained that I was on a *Haflinger pony* at a dressage show. The only mount less respectable might have been a broomstick horse. Like the two riders who smashed into me, you may wonder what on earth I was doing there.

The truth is that I have a long history of pulling for underdogs. And Marcoe the tiny cream colored stallion definitely fit that bill. So, I agreed to compete him for my student, thinking the worse outcome might include some staring, point-ing, and laughing from other riders. Mostly I was right on this account, except we encountered **a lot** of staring and laughing.

But the beauty of this scenario lies in the fact that this hairy, chunky, charming pony has no clue he is the most atypical dressage competitor in the state. He has the heart of a lion and loyalty of a best friend. He doesn't realize that our fellow riders in the warm-up arena stare at him not for his good looks but because they're pondering *what is that pony doing here?* In his mind, they stare because he's so like-able and handsome. Thus, the more they stare, the bouncier he trots, as if to show off for them what his short legs can do. The more he bounces, the more his fuzzy untamed mane flies around, which invites more staring.

In fact, riders stare at us without shame from under the brims of their top hats, as if their parents never taught them not to stare. They crane their necks with mouths open and look confused, like maybe they are the ones in the wrong place, not me.

Briefly, they contemplate snubbing us for being such a spectacle in their stuffy competition setting. But at the end of the day, it's hard to hate Marcoe and me. We're having such a good time that I'm grinning, chatting, and waving at folks, lightening the mood a little in the warm-up arena. And Marcoe, well, that little guy is just darn cute. Impossibly cute, actually. He melts your heart and he knows it.

He also knows that he *refuses* to be beat by fancier competition, no matter if he is one third its size. When he enters the dressage arena, the little guy is all business. He gives every performance 150 percent of his effort and, shockingly, it has paid off. The handsome pony won his share of blue ribbons last year, beating competitors that he stood no chance of beating. After all, most of his blue ribbons stand taller than he does. Along the way, Marcoe has acquired quite a fan club. He's taken on rock star status. A dozen or more total strangers come to watch us compete now at shows, marveling at this unlikely star and commenting on his wild mane. They take pictures and bring him carrots. They clap and cheer and run up to us after each class.

Marcoe loves the attention. He *deserves* it, too, which is why I have been attempting to take things a lot more seriously even if I am on a *pony* at a *dressage show*. I'm trying at least to take things as seriously as Marcoe does. I've stopped waving to friends and shouting hello and am instead focusing on the perfection of my aids and accuracy of my riding. I can feel my little half-horse fill up with pride under me.

Yes, riders and judges still stare at us. But try as they may to be annoyed by us, they just can't. Staring at us, their constipated show nerves dissipate. They forget to be so uptight and worried for a moment. They relax for a second and not knowing what else to do, they actually smile back. Any minute, they'll start to have some fun. And, who knows, maybe they'll add a fifth golden principle for competitors' behaviors at shows:

Don't pick on the little guy because he may kick your butt.

Calling Hollywood

IT WAS WITH a pause of humility this morning that I looked at myself in the tack room mirror. I mean, *really looked at myself.* Mud caked my chaps in thick furrows. Horse slobber dripped off my elbow, and several strands of long tail hairs stuck out from my jacket zipper. I pushed my rain-sodden hair off my forehead with fingers coated in molasses and oat debris.

In moments like these, when my unsightly appearance is beyond words, I like to reflect on how far removed the realities of the horse industry are from fairy-tale images in children's storybooks. Or Currier and Ives' paintings. Or *The Black Stallion* movies. You get the idea. The *real* facts of equestrian life are so unglamorous that I sometimes feel the need to blurt this out when I first introduce myself as a horse trainer to strangers. When asked what I do for a living, I want to answer "I train horses... but it's not as glamorous as you might think."

I like to ward off any misinterpretations that I am a well-coiffed, clean-pressed society gal with box seats at the Kentucky Derby before they get out of hand. In reality, I am just like every other trainer—covered in horse drool, reeking of hay and hooves, picking sand out of my scalp. In fact, we equestrians rarely—if ever—resemble the amusing images of us portrayed by artists and Hollywood.

This fact re-confirmed itself for me this morning when, after taking in my dismal appearance, I reflected on sadistic and bizarre competitions that my father used to compete in called Sleigh Rallies. Held in sub-zero New England winters, these frosty events involve several horse and sleigh combinations lurching around a judge in snowy circles. The objective: whoever does not freeze to death first or flip his sleigh over into the snow bank is deemed a winner. Other ways to get a winning edge include adorning your horse in lots of jingling bells and outfitting your sleigh with lap robes resembling large animals like bear and sheep. A regular competitor in these events to this day, my father recently sent me a Vermont calendar featuring a photograph of him competing in a Sleigh Rally. To an uneducated person, the picture probably looked idyllic. A dapper looking gentleman wrapped in fur and resembling a member of the Russian army promenades merrily through the snow in his horse-drawn sleigh. It's the stuff of Christmas carols and greeting cards. In real life, it's a whole different story.

A closer inspection of the photo reveals ice hanging from my father's beard and snow balled so thick in the soles of the horse's feet he can barely move. I'm guessing it was no warmer than 5 degrees Fahrenheit in that photo. It begs the question: who wants to be outside in that weather at a sporting event involving cold metal buckles, steamy perspiring beasts, and lots and lots of icy snow? This was glamour on the verge of being insufferable, which made you wonder what was glamorous about it in the first place.

As a kid, I was once talked into participating in one of these Sleigh Rallies. Or, more accurately, I was tossed into some one's sleigh and told to go drive in the "Junior Driver" class for participants under 16 years old. I was 11 and had never piloted a sleigh. I was blathering in protest. Nobody seemed to care. The pony's owner tossed me the reins, slapped him on the butt, and next thing I knew, the judge was evaluating me. Within moments, my eyelashes collected snow, blurring my vision. My nose ran and I resorted to wiping it with my coat sleeve. My butt cheeks froze to the seat and my hands formed into such rigid claws around the reins that I couldn't have let go if I wanted to. In the end, I won the class for the simple fact that the pony went on auto-pilot and I sat in a state of frozen misery.

A photographer wanted to take a picture of me and the pony with our blue ribbon and my clattering teeth prevented me from protesting, even though I knew what a dismal photo we'd make. The pony's sweat froze to his rump in frosty streaks while my still running nose froze to my chin in an icicle. I thought how cruel it would be if this image ended up on anyone's Christmas card.

If Hollywood had portrayed that day, though, the pony and I would have been the centerpiece of a joyful, fashionable scene, taking part in a pastime reserved only for the very fortunate or very wealthy. My drippy nose and frostbitten extremities would have been blotted out with photo editing software. Fact and fiction would have collided yet again to fool a good many people into believing equestrians are a glamorous lot.

I knew the real truth, though. I felt it down into my frozen toes and chapped lips: I was doing something reserved for the very foolish. And someday I would make an entire career out of it.

The movie industry, though, still prefers its own (read as "faulty") interpretation of us horse trainers. Its leading lady (presumably someone like myself) always wins her race and looks radiant and beautiful afterwards. When disasters do happen, her horse manages to recover miraculously from a debilitating injury. Her clients are always jovial and purchasing horses of the caliber of Secretariat or Seabiscuit. And of course nobody is ever dirty—they are coiffed, pressed, and steamed.

Hollywood and booksellers could do me a favor by printing a disclaimer alongside their materials. It might say: *None of what you're about to see or read is true in real life. Truthfully, horse trainers are always covered in dirt and they smell funny. Where horses are involved, things are always going wrong and not much is glamorous. There's constantly a strange illness or injury to figure out, mares being hormonal, clients causing drama, trainers having meltdowns, etc.*

In fact, I think I'll go contact Hollywood this very moment. While I'm at it, I'm going to suggest a movie script that more accurately portrays the life of a horse trainer. I'll suggest Jennifer Aniston to star as me. I can't wait to see how she looks with alfalfa slobber in her hair or frozen snot on her chin.

A Sport without Underdogs

GROWING UP, I loved to watch Olympic coverage on T.V., especially the track and field events where sometimes a nobody from a little known country might sprint out of obscurity on her own two feet and topple a field of preferred athletes. I savored these come-from-behind scenarios, and cherished them more if the runner had overcome major life challenges to get there. You know, like poverty or broken limbs or genocide, that sort of stuff.

So much thrill and excitement followed these races. Sports announcers went wild into their microphones, newspapers clamored for the story, television news would broadcast the footage over and over in slow motion. And in mere seconds, a single moment in sports was carved in history. A previously unknown athlete with no Nike sponsorships or other endorsements had written her ticket to the top of her sport. I remember walking away from the television with a warm glow of inspiration inside my chest as if I, too, could someday blast out of a rural town in Vermont into the history books.

It's curious now to find myself in the world of dressage—a sport with no underdogs. During primetime coverage of this past month's dressage World Cup in Las Vegas, I reflected on how anti-climactic these big events can be when there are positively no come-from-behind moments in the sport, or unlikely candidates competing alongside the big names. I mean, who has ever seen a Welsh Cob at the Olympics? Or a rider from Belarus on the medal podium? When has a Bashkir Curly horse ever shown up in a Grand Prix test? Now, that would be cool.

Don't get me wrong. I'm not denouncing modern Grand Prix dressage competitors who have worked long and hard to claim their accomplishments. I'm just saying that if every now and then a Shetland pony actually ended up on the winner's podium, dressage competitions would be a lot more... well, exciting. We'd get announcers yelping into their microphones rather than droning in hushed librarian-like tones. We'd have spectators showing up in dozens, wondering which underdog might make a run on the first place ribbon—the Appaloosa, the Arabian cross, or the Fjord pony. We'd finally get some news coverage and little boys and girls saying they wanted to grow up to be dressage riders. Wouldn't this be different? If nothing else, it would definitely change the landscape of modern competitions.

As is, the only time I find myself saying "Holy cow! How about that?" is while watching an upper level stallion blow up in the warm-up arena, clearing out other horses and riders like bowling pins, rather than when an unlikely candidate turns in an impressive performance and WINS. The only excitement or unpredictability comes when high winds pick up and horses start losing their marbles. The only spectators that come to endure the hermetic silence at dressage venues are family members who have been threatened/cajoled/arm-twisted to be there. Wouldn't it be refreshing to have them come willingly because there were some storylines to follow (like the Chincoteague pony that used to live in the wild and is now going head to head with the top-ranked dressage horse/rider in this country?)

By its nature, dressage is a sport for all. It was developed to improve the training and performance of any horse, regardless of breed, talent, or Olympic potential. And for that reason, riders of all abilities and financial means undertake it as a hobby in this country, many of them with lofty competitive aims. The caveat, though, is that in theory a horse need not have Olympic potential to participate in dressage. When it actually comes to the Olympics or World Cup, though, you darn better get the right horse. I might be unpopular for saying it, but in dressage, someone who rides a $10,000 Welsh-Arab cross is very simply never going to pull off a feat like the relatively unknown runner Wilma Rudolph in the 1960 Rome Olympics, sprinting on a sprained ankle to become the first American woman to win 3 gold medals in a single Olympics. Rudolph had overcome a premature birth, polio, scarlet fever, whooping cough, and measles.

During last summer's Olympics, I watched with glee as a 16-year old member of the Brazilian dressage team competed aboard her plump Lusitano stallion—a total oddball for such levels of this sport. Maybe I hoped for the equestrian version of Rudolph. Luiza Tavares de Almeida performed nearly flawlessly. I held my breath, sort of like you would for a girl of modest means from one of those Balkan countries doing her floor routine in gymnastics. The Brazilian gal turned in an incredible ride, her perfectly obedient steed huffing and puffing his way through the test. I couldn't wait to see her score, hoping she'd make the cut for final rounds.

It was one of the lowest scores I've ever seen in an Olympics. And, see, that's my point. How exciting would it have been if this gal stood a real chance of scoring well and getting into the top ranks. How many dressage announcers would have jumped out of their chairs? Darn it, dressage might have even made it into mainstream news for a moment or two. Other riders with plump unfavored breeds of horses might show up at competitions and that would be... well, fun.

Ever since my 8th grade English report on Wilma Rudolph, I've always had a picture of her with me, either taped to a wall or close at hand someplace. Strategically squinting my eyes regarding reality, I just can't let go of this notion that sports should be a place for everyone. Dressage included. Maybe one day in my lifetime, things will change drastically and our sport, too, will suddenly have underdogs! And story lines! And hype from sports announcers! Just to be prepared, I'm in the market for an Olympic caliber Chincoteague-Bashkir Curly cross. One with really bizarre markings would be preferred. And one that can do an excellent victory lap.

So Much for Savvy

My father claims he was pouring out his heart the other day when my cell phone cut out and he realized he was talking to himself. I find this hard to believe for two reasons.

First, my father's version of pouring out his heart means reminding me that his property taxes are way too high. Secondly, being a horse trainer himself, my father knows that we equine professionals are nearly always in areas with spotty cell phone coverage. Therefore, one should never pour out one's heart to a trainer on a cell phone.

The cell phone issue has amused me for several years now, mainly because these little technological devices present an anomaly for us horse folks. You see, the average horse trainer is eccentric, introverted, and socially isolated. That's part of the reason we train horses; we don't fit into any other type of employment. Days filled by activities with non-verbal animals suit us perfectly.

Then along came cell phones. Suddenly, our days of talking only to ourselves, our dogs, or our horses now included a ringing telephone with real live people on the other end. Our social isolation went out the door. Our introverted ways were being challenged as human conversations infiltrated our tasks. We now conducted dialogues with prospective clients while sitting on a hay bale or bathing horses. We called in feed deliveries while mucking stalls.

In essence, we were no different than corporate executives. The glory of whole afternoons spent swatting flies and contemplating what sized saddle to put on the new Arabian in training was fleeting. Inevitably, we'd soon resemble corporate managers in other ways, like running to Starbucks at 4pm every day and talking too fast and shining our shoes.

For most of us, the transition looked a little awkward. It presented the opportunity for us to become bona fide *businesspeople*, a venture we trainers have been reticent to embrace. Moreover, technological concepts like "cell coverage," "bandwidth," or "web browsing" all seemed terribly advanced and tedious in the face of issues like whether Timothy or alfalfa hay is best at this time of year. Personally, I'd rather determine if the brand of fly spray I'm currently using on my steeds is actually working than try to figure out what key on my cell phone will create the letter "Q" in a text message.

In spite of our hesitation, most of us trainers do want to become more business savvy and cell phones seemed like they might lead us in that direction. I can count on one hand (with all fingers closed in a fist) how many trainers I know who actually make a decent living in this industry. Multiply that figure (0) by 10 and that's the number I know barely squeaking by. So, as you can see, we're still at zero for the number of horse training professionals able to a.) pay their electricity bills, b.) fuel up their diesel truck, AND c.) buy groceries. If we all possessed a bit more business savvy, that figure might change. So, maybe a half dozen trainers would suddenly make a decent living. Then, that half dozen can share its secrets with the rest of us. And before you know it, we horse trainers won't be so broke.

Those annoying cell phones seemed like the first step in this chain. After we figured out how to clip them onto our riding pants and Wranglers, we were pretty excited about them. Some of us went as far as printing up business cards highlighting our cell phone number. An evolution was at hand. Horse trainers with business cards? This was unheard of, and yet here we were reaching into our shirt pockets and handing out these handy slips of paper. Then, we mastered the art of *answering* the cell phone when potential clients called. This proved to be no easy task. Using one hand to press a phone to your ear leaves only one hand free to wrangle with a rearing colt, when sometimes you need no fewer than four hands for this.

To this day, my good buddy Mark is the only trainer I've witnessed be able to peel an orange, answer his phone, and control a rearing colt all at the same time. He's also the one who proved to me after all these years that, regardless of handy cell phones, we horse trainers just aren't cut out to be business savvy. Who were we kidding? We don't know how to market ourselves (or even what this means). We have a hard time caring about "customer relations." We're impossible to work for (just ask our employees). And Turbo Tax sounds to us like the name of an oxer in a jump course.

Eventually, those cell phones that held temporary promise of leading us into more profitable lifestyles took on other purposes. We still use them when we're sitting on hay bales, but we don't talk to prospective clients anymore. We're back to our afternoons of swatting flies, talking to our dogs… and playing the occasional video game on our phone. With the invention of sleeker and more technological phones, we trainers are now spending more time entertaining ourselves than trying to balance our saggy checkbooks.

My buddy Mark and I were at a horse show recently when he pulled out a new high tech cell phone that resembled a hockey puck. It looked like something you'd carry with you on Wall Street, only it promised features that appealed to horse professionals like him and I. The new phone, he explained, was guaranteed to be more or less indestructible.

"Watch this!," he said as he hurled it against the side of a metal barn. The phone bounced off and flew into a pile of sawdust. Mark then ran over and jumped up and down on top of it with his steel-toed boots. It was waterproof, weather-proof, and vehicle-proof, meaning that Mark could drive over it with his diesel truck, which he had of course already tried repeatedly. He had also submerged it in water troughs and left it in his horse trailer to endure extreme heat just to see what might happen. So far, the phone proved indestructible. The following day, he intended to test its survival under a set of tractor tires, he told me like a giddy child with a new toy.

In that moment, I understood how cell phones had become such an integral part of trainers' lives, even though they didn't lead us to being business savvy. They *did*, however, give us something to try crushing under our tractors.

Could you Point me in the Direction of Civilization?

W E WERE LONG past that point of exhaustion when everything seems funny and yet our failure to find a store was really not funny. My groom and I, in need of a few items like water and duct tape for the show we were attending, had driven around for nearly 40 minutes passing nothing but tract homes and barren fields drying out in 100 degree heat. Surely, any moment, we would pass a gas station or a 7-Eleven or a supermarket or at the very least a roadside fruit stand. But nothing. We drove endlessly in our bubble of air conditioning finding not so much as a can of iced tea.

Our agitation stirred up as we admitted aloud to each other that we expected this. We were, after all, at one of the large shows held at a facility in the deserted valley between Sacramento, CA and the Sierra foothills. It's a no-man's land, populated by a handful of retirees who can handle the heat and apparently enjoy living on a flat plain void of trees or stores selling goods that facilitate human survival. Things like food and band-aids, ice and towels and string.

In our disgruntled—and very thirsty—state, we returned to the showgrounds to sit on overturned buckets in the blazing sun and wait for the day to end. Twirls of sand occasionally blew up in our faces, adhering to our sweaty skin and causing me to wonder how I'd ever squeeze into my competition gear for the last class of the afternoon. The equation of sweat+dirt+skin tight clothing made me want to run off and find a different job. It's moments like these that make me wonder why I chose horse training as a profession over, say, banking or designing or something civilized.

But the larger question for me was why on earth do people organize horse shows in California in the least desirable places? If you're going to invite participants to come be hostage at your event for five consecutive days, at least make sure your venue is some place people actually want to go. My grumpiness on this matter derives, as most things do, from my New England upbringing. Back East, where land is more affordable and large horse facilities proliferate the countryside, horse shows were always held just outside charming little villages. So, if you found yourself gritting it out to finish a class during a torrential downpour one minute, you could then be sitting in a cozy breakfast nook having a warm scone 5 minutes later. A friendly waitress calling you "honey" might inquire why you look so sodden and bring you a complimentary warm beverage. And should you need some duct tape or band-aids or string, you will find them within 25 steps of your scone at the main street hardware store.

Every summer through my youth, my dad and I traveled all over the Northeast for Combined Driving competitions. I served as his groom, traveling companion, and cheerleader. We went to New York, Connecticut, New Jersey, Pennsylvania—the same circuit of shows every season. After the first couple seasons, we had our favorite stomping grounds in every horse show town. In Massachusetts, we liked to go to the Blue Bonnet Diner for mid-afternoon hot chocolates and a break from the bustle of the showgrounds. In Pennsylvania, we hit the Iron Skillet every morning for gigantic breakfasts that kept us fueled all day. In Connecticut, we knew exactly where to stop for ice, supplies, and carrots for the horses. Whenever dad broke something on his carriage or harness, we knew who to call and where to go. And any time we wanted to just sit down and take a break, we knew the best places in all those charming villages. We knew where to get the best croissant or berry pie slice, the best quiet bookstore, the best outdoor park where we could nap in the grass. Sometimes, these things were vital to a good performance at the show. I grew up naively assuming it was all part of competing horses.

Then I moved to California.

Land is a precious commodity here in California, the largest available amounts of it existing in far-flung deserted areas. And these deserted areas during mid-summer show season tend to be so hot that many folks get heat stroke just from standing around. Less of them might fall victim if there were cozy stores nearby where one could duck out of the elements for a moment or grab a buttery scone after morning classes. But there are none of those. No shops, no stores, no villages. Just a horse show venue sticking up in the midst of these flat bone-dry plains. Some days, I've wandered around so long looking for a single tree under which I could sit and shade myself that I've nearly missed my class. I've finally realized that trees just don't grow in hot barren plains and therefore gotten used to that sizzling skin-scorched feeling on my forehead and cheeks.

On this particular day of failing to find a store, as if one might miraculously appear on our hundredth search, my groom and I pondered aloud about the oddity of the scene. The mercury pushed past 100-degrees, dust swirled, horses wilted. And the show went on. Participants tried their best to present themselves glamorously with polished black boots and shiny saddles, but the glamour fleeted quickly. Within five minutes of all the polishing, everything was drenched in sweat, filmed in dust. Ladies' makeup melted and dribbled down their starched collars, making pink and blue stripes from eyelids to ribcage. Wet rings blossomed under their arms, triangles of moisture pressed through the backs of their show jackets. The horses huffed and puffed, their sleek coats turning to foamy lather.

I dreaded my own class within an hour and the temperature by then well over 100. To assuage my bitter mood, my groom reminded me that things weren't that bad. They could be worse, after all. Remember Woodinville? With that, I almost fell off my bucket.

A year ago, we'd gone to an early spring show in Woodinville, a town that maps describe as "historical." After spending 72 hours there, I discovered that historical is a euphemism for "place you never want to visit." I entered town via Main Street, where all the buildings seem to have emptied out at the turn of the 20th century, and promptly locked my car doors. I couldn't tell if I'd somehow driven onto the set of a creepy Hollywood movie or if the place was for real, but nonetheless, the town—if I can call it that—sent out bad vibes in every direction.

Block after block was filled with abandoned stone buildings rotting into the earth. I passed one or two other cars carrying folks trying to figure out the quickest route out of there. For miles, I passed shuttered saloons, deserted storefronts, and crumbling facades, all of which were surrounded by acres of scorched plains baking in the heat. In fact, the temperatures that weekend held steady at 112 degrees and all I fantasized about was a cold bottle of Gatorade. My horses fell sick from the heat and my car broke down, but all I could think about was a cold Gatorade. For 72 hours, I dreamt of getting the hell out of Woodinville and its ghostly downtown and sitting down in a patch of shade with a cold drink.

On this particular day, my groom was right. Things could have been worse. My makeup might melt down my shirtfront and I would undoubtedly contract some minor heatstroke by day's end, but at least we weren't in Woodinville. We would get by without the towels and ice and string we searched for earlier. Then, like delirious souls clamoring towards a desert mirage, we will tell stories about our favorite aisle in Target. Oh, Target. What we wouldn't give right then for a place like that with bonafide signs of civilization! Then, my groom will listen politely as I reminisce for the billionth time about those charming little horse show villages in my youth.

Does Anyone Know What Day It Is?

L AST WEEK, I woke up in a strange bed and tried to recall what day it was. Aha! I remembered that I had to ride a young horse in the Materiale class at 3pm and therefore it must be Saturday. Working my way back from that information, I determined that we were in the month of July, I must be in the town of Woodside (where the show was being held), and I was therefore in a bed at my friend's house in a nearby town. I rolled over to see who or what might be sharing the bed with me and met the stare of a green eyed Bengal.

Welcome to the life of a horse trainer. We equine professionals spend so much time on the road that entire weeks blur together. In fact, I don't even remember June of this year. Is it possible that leap years eliminate whole months? Anyway, I sometimes think the life of a traveling circus performer or rock band might even be more stable than what we horse trainers have.

Waking up in strange beds next to someone else's pets has become a comfortable norm. I've shared couches, mattresses, and futons so far with dozens of Border collies and German shepherds, rambunctious cats and poodles, a turtle, baby chickens, a blind parrot, and one particularly high-strung whippet. They've all taken me in as part of their family. Lest I forget how odd my lifestyle is, I sometimes remind myself that other women my age tuck their children into bed at night and then read a book or settle down to sleep with their partners. I, meanwhile, peel back the bed sheets in an unfamiliar room and crawl onto the tiny section of mattress that has been left for me by the whippet.

I was giving a clinic recently on the coast in California after a five-day stretch of teaching and competing in different towns when a gentleman asked me where I live. I couldn't remember the last time I slept in my own bed. I hesitated to give this person an answer, fearing I might be lying to indicate I had a real *home*. I mean, one with my *own* pet staring at me in the morning.

"My car?" I replied, thinking that might be the most accurate address to give.

He raised an eyebrow and said my web site stated that I live in Santa Cruz, California. Was that no longer true?, he asked, glancing towards my two-door Toyota the way you'd look at a homeless woman's cart of belongings.

"Oh yeah. Well, yes, I have a P.O. box there," I answered. And a bed, I thought, although I hadn't visited it in so long that I couldn't guarantee its existence right then.

"In theory, yes, I do live there... if I were ever there, that is."

You see, the nice gentleman fell into the category of people who don't own horses and are unfamiliar with the lifestyle necessary to sustain oneself in this industry. I attended a party last night with several other such folks. Pleasant innocent people who "ooh and ahh" when they hear I train horses for a living. Their eyes widen, their mouths turn up into giddy smiles. I know what they're thinking, these people who have to work in offices all day under fluorescent lights. They think I lead the most glamorous life on the planet.

Wow, they think, she works with horses all day! Of course, to them this means that I live in a world much like the one portrayed in *National Velvet*. I wear fancy hats with feathers in them. I drink mint juleps every day at 4pm. I have a stable boy who lives to polish my boots and wrap my horses' legs. I gallop like Lady Godiva through lush green countryside in the late mornings. All while collecting a paycheck.

"It sounds more glamorous than it is," I admitted to the party-goers, wondering if the goo on my right arm was dried horse slobber or fly spray. Little do they know I've never had a mint julep in my life and I think the last time I galloped through lush green countryside was in 1996. And it was an unintentional gallop; the horse was running away with me. Whether or not this counts as a luckier lifestyle than a fluorescent-lit office worker's, I'm still undecided.

But I can live for weeks out of one suitcase, and like most horse people, I can sleep positively anywhere. I may not immediately know where I am when I wake up, but I can usually toggle together those details after a cup of coffee and a phone call to my groom. This involves a quick trip to the trunk of my car where I keep my phone charger and life-on-the-road survival kit: coffee, instant oatmeal, socks for all seasons, chapstick, business cards, and antibacterial wipes.

A few weeks ago, I was driving down a highway somewhere here in California when my mother called. I felt a bit groggy from shaking off the previous day's heat exhaustion, horse show fatigue, and general weariness. Nonetheless, I was leaving a horse event in one town for another event in a town a few hours away. Characteristically chipper, my mom asked where I was.

I looked at the road signs and then at the brown hillsides. Then, I looked at the other cars on the road with me. Embarrassingly, an answer did not present itself immediately. I forgot for a moment if I were leaving a horse event or heading to another one, or both.

"You know, Mom, I'm not really sure," came my answer. "Hopefully, I'll figure it out by the time I get where I'm going."

What Are YOU Looking At?

ANIMAL LOVER OR not, every rider has endured a hair-raising, nail-biting moment of time when her life flashed before her eyes due to a wildlife critter that would normally seem adorable and charming. But in these moments, wildlife seems like one of life's great cruelties and someone like myself—an 18-year vegetarian—may consider taking up arms for hunting season to settle the score with a wild turkey that scuttled out from a bush and spooked my horse.

I had one such ride this morning, which got me thinking about this. Afterwards, I felt like I needed to go to the local ASPCA chapter or wildlife protection agency and apologize for the 15 minutes I spent cursing profanely at a majestic male deer that nearly ended my life. Normally, a six-point buck perched atop a foggy cliff would incite a flutter in my heart and even inspire a verse or two of haiku poetry. But he's the last thing I want to see when I am on a horse that instantly turns into a fear-crazed, runaway lunatic.

Let me give a disclaimer here before going any further that I personally love wildlife. I am a dues-paying member of Sierra Club, I mountain bike and hike regularly, and I take time every day to stop and ponder the sheer wonder of Mother Nature. However, when I am on a horse, I often curse the fuzzy and furry members of the forest. It is fair to say I even shout and sometimes think about throwing things at them. Were it the case that my horse did not gallop away and jeopardize my mortal existence, I would definitely view them otherwise. Yes, the leaping jackrabbits, startling deer, and darting birds would be met with a friendly "aw, aren't you cute?" rather than "I'm gonna kill you! Get OUTTA here!"

Anyway, back to this morning's ride. I was precariously convincing a feisty three-year old mare that even though the other horses were eating their breakfasts and she was grumpy, we still needed to get some work done. I had a hard time selling her on this. After a few laps around the arena, she was looking to convince me that her grumpiness was going nowhere and I should take her back to the barn. She pinned her ears, swished her tail, spooked at a few things here and there. Basically, she made my job of riding her dismal.

About 20 minutes later, though, she began to come around. She started to go through her paces rather nicely in fact, so I asked her to pick up a brisk ground-covering canter (a risky move with a young horse on a chilly morning!), which she did promptly. I began to smile like a proud teacher. And then I glanced up the hill outside our arena. There in the mist stood a very large buck looking straight down at us. I gritted my teeth. The mare hadn't seen him yet; she was still performing beautifully, although I knew the second she saw him, it would be over for me. She would take the opportunity to bolt wildly and throw some wretched antics at me, re-starting her campaign to be done with riding for the day. Shoot! We were already in a rather speedy canter. Once she laid eyes on that muscular fellow with the antlers, she would hit the speed of light. And I would either be in the dirt or saying prayers.

So I started to do the only thing I could do. "GET OUTTA HERE!" I snarled. No movement. In fact, the big guy seemed more interested in us now. My mare kept cantering along, miraculously not yet noticing him. In fact, she kept things far cooler than I in that moment as I launched into a verbal tirade.

"Go ON! Git! Go away! Get outta here you blasted fool... do you want me killed? Don't you have some deer harem you need to get back to? Why are you looking at me? WHAT? Get outta here. Why are you just STANDING there?" My screams echoed off rocks and down canyons. It lifted up into tree tops and skimmed across mud puddles. I admitted to myself that I probably appeared like someone recently escaped from an asylum and not meant to be on horseback. But I didn't mind if anyone standing nearby wanted to label me a crazy person. I just plain didn't care because I was determined to finish this ride still on the back of my horse, not in the dirt.

Finally, the giant antlers turned the other direction and he trotted off to pester something else. I felt myself start breathing again. My mare kept cantering and I smiled at her. What a delightful ride we were having. And that was what mattered, right? Who cared if I momentarily became a crazy person who shouted at furry adorable forest animals? I would donate a few extra dollars to the Sierra Club.

Does this Spandex
Make me Look Fat?

UNFORTUNATELY, I'VE BECOME an avid cyclist in the past year. I say unfortunately because it's another activity that requires wearing a fair amount of Lycra.

It was bad enough coming home from the barn every day in my riding clothes and mustering the courage to stop for dinner fixings at a supermarket where invariably, some mid-30 year old guy asks "have you been out riding?" Which is how he excuses himself from staring at my backside in skin tight breeches. What Mr. Supermarket fails to realize is that NOBODY wants attention drawn to her in her riding clothes. Terribly outdated in style, uncomfortable, and awkward, riding clothes definitely rank at the bottom of the fashion ladder within the sporting world. To have someone staring at your backside while in this outfit simply adds insult to injury.

I used to think dismal fashions applied only to my discipline of dressage. But after closer inspection, I concluded that, no, the horse world in general looked straight out of Vaudeville.

So, whenever I start to lament the necessity of tight breeches for English riding, I go and watch a Western class at a show. Now, *those* riders have some funny outfits. Shiny belt buckles the size of dinner plates, enormous hats, gaudy shirts, flapping fringes dangling off nearly every surface from saddle to pants to gloves. To me, they look like they belong more in a parade or circus than in an equestrian competition. And this does my heart good because my outfit seems a lot less strange. My pants may be tighter, but at least they don't have fringes.

Of course, Western apparel pales in comparison to the cabaret styles in a Saddle Seat class. Probably not since the 1940s have so many people under one roof donned derbies and tailcoats. Neon-colored tailcoats, I might add, plus tapered pants that flare out at the bottoms to fall over pointed ankle boots. To me, these riders look like they've trotted straight out of the The Great Gatsby into the 21st century.

However, their styles might seem arguably modern compared to what carriage driving folks pull out of their closets. I grew up on the back of my father's carriage and I probably never stopped asking him the purpose of his lap robe or apron as drivers call them. Weren't aprons for kitchens? How did they contribute to one's driving skills? The cumbersome lap blankets were just part of the outfit, according to my Dad. Also part of the outfit was a funny looking straw hat, a blazer, and thick leather gloves.

Equestrian apparel easily surpasses my cycling uniforms in terms of absurdity. But it also has something really good going for it, in my opinion. Once you get past the discomfort of artificial fabrics and the fact that they cling to you in all the wrong places, riding apparel forces us to give up being so self-conscious. You get past any shyness about wearing tight clothes or looking silly, because after all, you're wearing the threads necessary to do what you love. This recognition also helps get your mind around the fact that a pair of riding breeches, which can fold up to fit in your palm, costs you $200 or more. After you've plunked down that much cash on a garment weighing about six ounces and likely made by children in China, you want to wear it as often as possible for return on investment. To do this, you adopt other activities in those breeches beyond just riding your horse. Thus, the errands to supermarket, bank, coffee shop.

To the uninitiated, riding pants appear to be nothing but glorified leggings from the Active Wear section of Walmart. But the uninitiated have likely never experienced the fragility of one's crotch after a couple hours in the saddle. Once they have had that unique feeling-like-none-other, they will concede that the invention of riding pants—no matter how ridiculous they look—was marvelous. For anyone with respect for his or her crotch, riding pants are unavoidable. Unlike leggings, sweat pants, or jeans, riding pants will never bunch up in one's crotch. That alone is worth $200 in my opinion. They will also never slide up over a rider's ankles and rub his calves into a bloody pulp. And they will never leave inseam bruises on one's private regions.

But what they *will* always do, guaranteed, is hug one's rear end tightly. This alone might not be such a problem if non-riders could spend less time staring. Or maybe the staring wouldn't be so bad without the rhetorical questions.

So, when Mr. Supermarket asks me "Have you been out riding?," I look him square in the eye and answer "Actually, no, I'm on my way to Vaudeville. If you'll pardon me, I need to go find my apron."

For Sale: Overpriced,
High-Strung, and Mostly Lame

GIVEN THAT WE'RE in the worst economic downturn most Americans have ever witnessed, I decided to face the situation head-on by sprawling on my couch and flipping through horse magazines while ignoring radio, news, and gloomy neighbors' forecasts about the crisis.

I knew equine media would provide me the obscurity I sought, because the horse world excels at distancing itself from fiscal norms and realities. So, yes, while unemployment rates in the U.S. surge higher day to day, banks collapse, and businesses capsize, the prices for horses are... going up. In a market where—logically—sale prices should be absurdly low, there is not a deal to be had. If I relied on the equine industry for my bearings, I would be led to believe we're actually in financially lush times where money is spilling in abundance from Americans' pockets.

This confusion is nothing new. The horse market is one that makes zero sense and likely never will. It follows no such thing as trends, measurable gains or losses, logic, or financial cycles. In fact, I'm recounting the typical pattern followed by my students when they decide to buy their first horses. They each set out on a shopping spree with specific requirements such as wanting only a male horse, 10 years old, extensive training, black in color, priced around $5,500. A week later, they return with a three-year old mare possessing no training, unless you count the four times it bucked off its current trainer, with a $12,000 price tag. When I point out that the new acquisition is neither trained nor sane and then query about the logic behind its purchase, my client will have no answer except that she fell in love with the horse. And the next minute, she was writing a check.

This horse, which will prove impossible to ride, will cost the proud owner roughly $50,000 in board fees over the next ten years. And here's the thing: unlike real estate and vintage cars, horses don't gain value. So, the costly untrained horse will be worth even *less* ten years later. The new—and now poor—owner will eventually sell this horse for $1,200. Anyone with an ounce of financial savvy will shake her head at this scenario, devastated by such a hard luck story. But truly this is a common story in the horse world, which keeps daring somebody, *anybody*, to figure out its logic.

For sellers, this lack of rationality spells good news because it allows them during times like this to charge staggering sums for four-legged steeds without talent or beauty. While flipping through my horse magazines, I stopped to contemplate a photo of a horse for sale that, all kidding aside, had such a dysfunctional body that I couldn't tell for a moment which was the front end and which the rear. The price on this beauty? $9,500. Its seller indicated the price was a steal in this suffering economy. I held off calling her to suggest, first, that she re-evaluate the definition "a steal" and, second, that she donate the horse to a petting zoo because it would be the best home for him.

At the end of the day, though, it will be her and not me with advice to give. This seller obviously knows her way around this bizarre horse economy. Her phone will ring soon and the caller will say he's looking for a bay colored, 16-hand Anglo-Arabian with competition experience, but within a week that same caller will be loading her midget 14-hand unregistered and untrained brown horse into his trailer with a money order payable for the full amount.

A year later, the fellow will probably return the horse to her without refund, explaining that it just didn't work out for him. He will swallow the $9,500 he initially paid, an additional $4,000 in board fees, and $1,300 in vet and farrier costs. Then, odds favor him repeating the whole scenario within six months—purchasing an unsuitable horse for $9,000 or more, dumping time and money into him, and then either giving him away for free or re-selling him for $1,500.

Meanwhile, the seller of the original untrained unattractive brown horse I saw last week will gladly accept the cost-free return of her horse, because soon her phone will ring again and she will sell the horse for $10,500 this time around (because he now has a year of training, compliments of the fellow who returned him). It ends up being a sweet deal. She gets to profit twice on the unattractive horse with no talent or beauty and escapes paying a whole year of his feed and upkeep expenses. It's ingenious in an unexplainable way.

For anyone who's genuinely downtrodden about this economic downturn, I'd like to offer up my couch and this pile of horse magazines as therapy. A few minutes immersed in horse economics will leave you feeling so perplexed that you'll forget your woes. By the way, I know of a horse with relatively no talent for sale. I am offering him for a bargain (read as: $10,000) and can assure that you'll be able to tell his front end from his hind (read as: he's not attractive beyond that) and he will make someone a good investment (read as: you'll be able to sell him at a major loss in five years). Please call if you are interested.

Walk Like Me, Talk Like Me

Anyone who has spent much time around a training barn or at horse shows recognizes quickly that a trainer's most valuable asset is what I like to call his groupies. These folks comprise the small cloud that follows him around, always close at his heels and aware of every move, much like the syncopated block of musicians in a marching band.

When the trainer sits down, his groupies cluster around in nearby chairs. When the trainer acts busy, the swarm in turn flusters off in various directions to occupy themselves. And so it goes. They are like a loyal shadow, mirroring the trainer, propping up his ego, laughing at his less-than-funny jokes, and marveling at his unparalleled skill with horses. And they pay him for the opportunity to do this.

You see, groupies are important and worth cultivating because in large measure, they are an extension of us trainers and whatever impression they give the industry is, for better or for worse, how the industry then sees us. This can obviously work in a trainer's favor, or to his detriment.

As a trainer, you hope for well-heeled groupies, not to mentioned well-behaved ones. At shows, you picture the cloud that follows you as a fashionable ensemble of sophisticated tastes and articulate speech. You hope for a tidily groomed batch of grateful and polite individuals, eager to help each other out, support other competitors, and occasionally stroke your ego by saying you're the best rider they've seen on in decades. When they stock your cooler with your favorite snacks and beverages, consider it an added bonus.

Equating you with the quality of your groupies, fellow trainers and competitors immediately elevate you to a level that would take years to achieve by sheer hard work, good training, and a successful show record. Your colleagues and prospective clients automatically assume that, judging from the caliber of your groupies, you must surely ride only the best horses, collect top dollar for your services, and speak with deep wisdom on every topic.

In fact, groupies are so pivotal in the status of our careers that I've witnessed shrewd trainers focus their efforts on cultivating groupies more than on training horses. Instead of riding horses all day, they put their efforts into schmoozing over coffee, making phone calls, and managing their image. They often end up earning far more money than the rest of us who are trying to make it to the top with pure hard work. It's like the Enron business model applied to the horse world.

What the average trainer usually ends up with, however, is quite different than a uniformly well-heeled group of loyalists. There are generally at least a handful of questionable seeds in the mix. And as I've said, these characters do far more for your reputation than your talent, skill, or show record.

I recall an episode at a Regional Championship competition that all too clearly illustrated this fact for me. The loudspeaker paged me to the show office—a cluttered nexus of paperwork run by over-worked grey-haired ladies and occupied by nervous competitors. Certain that I had handled every detail of my entry forms and stabling payments, I couldn't immediately imagine what business I possibly needed to attend to in the office. So, I took my time casually wandering over there.

By the time I arrived, not only was the loudspeaker paging me for a third time, but a small army of horse show officials in golf carts had been dispatched to come haul me in. Worse, I heard a distinct commotion inside the office long before I got near the door. There was yelling and crying. There was name-calling. There were hostile over-worked grey-haired ladies. It sounded bad, very bad. And I had a nagging suspicion that the source for the commotion, and the explanation for my being paged and the golf cart brigade, was one of my students.

I swung open the door and, yes, there stood one of my own. Apparently, she had taken it upon herself to go straighten out some paperwork in the show office (ignoring strict instructions from me never to go anywhere on her own, lest she go off like a loose cannon as she was now), and nobody seemed to know what prompted it, but she was now in the midst of a hysterical breakdown. Perhaps it was the stress of needing to put signatures on a few entry forms. Or deciding between entering her horse in a class on Saturday versus Sunday. Who knew. She was now choking and shuddering for breath, throwing papers around the office, her eyes were bloodshot.

The other competitors unfortunate enough to be in the show office had smeared themselves against the walls, much like at a high school dance where pimply teenagers try to blend into the furnishings. In this case, they tried to stay out of arm's reach from my now-crazed client. The ladies running the office stood aghast, like four helpless deer paralyzed by headlights. They had contemplated whether to call the police, the state mental hospital, or me. Obviously, they settled on me. They had decided this spasmodic emotional eruption was my problem, let me deal with it.

In the end, I did somewhat deal with it. With the help of my cowboy friend, we physically extracted the wailing woman in question from the office, restrained her in a horse stall, and outlined for her why she was never again allowed in the horse show office. Given the extent of her distress and flailing, I considered our efforts heroic. However, they did nothing to erase the episode from history.

To this day, fellow competitors still talk about that "horse show office meltdown" as if it's an affliction that could claim anyone at the least expected time. Nobody wants to be the groupie that defects and loses her wits in public. And from personal experience, I can tell you that no trainer wants to be remembered for the time she slung a blathering adult woman over her shoulder and carried her out of the office. That falls into the category of hard work, too hard. The Enron business model looks a lot more enticing.

You Want Me to Do... What?

JUST TO MAKE things confusing for clients, the equine industry fails to uphold a generalized standard for the cost of training and lesson fees. The result is that customers often have no idea why they're paying so much, or so little, for services. Rates can range from plain affordable to eye-popping outrageous. And unlike in other service industries, the horse world maintains no clear correlation between a trainer's experience, qualifications, and salary. It's all very random.

However, possession of one particular asset does seem to ensure a trainer's ability to charge—and receive—rather lofty figures. A foreign accent allows an instructor who might otherwise make $60 per lesson to charge over $100. It matters not whether the accent is Slovakian, Finnish, or German. Sometimes, even Canadian will do.

All that counts is that it hints of a person's roots being beyond U.S. soil. This fact alone gives any trainer a huge advantage in attracting equestrian clientele. His skills never need to be scrutinized; the foreign accent, along with a tidy riding outfit, leads to the assumption that he is in fact superior to domestic trainers. It's much like assuming that because someone is Japanese, he must be an expert of sushi. Riding and horsemanship have existed for so much longer overseas that we Americans tend to cling to foreigners as if their DNA is encoded with riding wisdom.

I myself was lured in by the centuries of dressage traditions in Europe and over the years have made not one, but twelve, pilgrimages to ride and train there. Honestly, I can't tell you that I learned any more there than I have from my trainers here in the U.S., but I did come away with a feeling of storybook magic—

cobbled barn courtyards, well-groomed horses, charming little indoor arenas, and well, all those accented lessons.

Following an instructor's orders during a lesson is difficult enough. But when you only marginally understand what he's saying, it's far worse.

One time in Portugal, my mother and I were being yelled at to "Sit cloze to zee wizards!" My mom tried to satisfy the instruction by riding her horse close to everything around—the fence railing, spectators, chairs. Our trainer kept yelling. Finally, Mom trotted her horse up alongside mine and through clenched teeth asked me, "Where the *hell* is the *wizard*?" I stifled a laugh. "Withers, Mom. Sit close to the horse's withers...."

At this, she huffed and puffed, "If he meant withers, why didn't he just say *withers*?"

"Well, he did, sort of. I mean, he tried." I answered.

"He should try *harder*."

I didn't entirely agree, knowing that sometimes when those with foreign accents try harder to pronounce something, they generally just end up yelling. A few minutes earlier, for instance, our Portuguese instructor told me to "cross ja geogonal." What? He wanted me to cross the what? GEOganal, he repeated louder this time. I figured I'd just keep cantering around him in a circle until I figured out what he wanted. **GEO**ganal, he shouted, this time waving his arms. GEOGANAL, GEOGANAL! By default, I eventually rode across the diagonal, which apparently is what he wanted because he stopped yelling his strange translation at me.

A few months earlier, I suffered my first introduction to such public embarrassment. In Germany, I convinced the revered trainer Egon von Neindorff, by then a very old and cynical man, to allow me the use of a translator for my lessons as I didn't speak German very well and old Neindorff refused to speak anything but his native tongue. An American journalist kindly sat in on my lesson, translating every comment Neindorff made to me, which wasn't much. His lesson went much like this:

"Trot.......good.......Walk......good....Circle....good."

Then, the translator got up to use the bathroom and the second she left the arena, Neindorff started spewing orders in rapid fire. Of course, I had no clue what the old codger was saying, so I just kept trotting my horse. This was obviously the wrong decision. Neindorff's voice escalated, he fired off instructions even faster, his eyes bulged. Panicked, I clenched by legs and held my breath, which must have been the cue for my mare to begin a lovely, if entirely unsolicited, piaffe.

There I sat atop this horse with legs moving wildly, and yet we were going nowhere. I poked with my spur, I clucked... and we went faster in place. She bounced up and down, working herself into a lather, and I could not get her to move forward. I was horrified. My face burned red. But then I noticed Neindorff had stopped shouting at me. I looked across the arena to see that he was doubled over, holding his stomach in laughter, so heartily humored by my spectacle that he was gasping for air.

I vowed then and there to never repeat this kind of scene. But I have to admit that I've not been successful. All these years later, I'm still befuddled.

Recently, my mentor—a Spaniard with Australian accent—unleashed his own very strange dialect in an order that went something like: "Now, mike aye twanty meh-ter half curcle." Confused, I just kept trotting (obviously having learned nothing from my previously mentioned German adventures) while he stared at me. He repeated his instruction, giving me the benefit of being hearing deficient. Then he stared more. After I trotted another four times around the arena, he asked wearily "Why you no do what I tell you?"

If only I *knew* what he told me.

Idiotic Idioms

I'VE BEEN PONDERING a couple of common phrases from the English language lately wondering what deceptive fool created them in the first place. You know when something gets repeated so many times that we start taking its literal meaning for granted? Assuming it ever had a literal meaning, that is.

Let's start with the misleading phrase "healthy as a horse."

In my everyday wanderings, I hear folks say that a person is "healthy as a horse" if he is, for instance, running marathons at 75 years old and has never suffered an ailment, prolonged sickness, or injury. This person is so genetically superior that in six and a half decades of life, he's never experienced even the most minor upset like indigestion, fatigue, toothache, or hair loss. And so, therefore, he is healthy as a horse, right?

Nothing could be further from the truth. The guy is a miracle and resembles equine well-being in no way, shape, or form. To be precise, if this gentleman were in fact healthy as a horse, he would have been lucky to live to his *tenth* birthday without a major medical procedure, never mind his 75th. If he were horse-like, he would have racked up thousands of dollars in medical bills and experimental treatments. He would have long ago become perilously ill from a fly bite or minor scrape on his leg, or mysteriously develop gastric distress after eating his routine meal of 20 years.

Anyone with horses knows what I'm getting at. Horses are the most fragile animals I've encountered, susceptible to bizarre fevers and split-second injuries. They can be in fine health one moment and then in a welted rash the next. Or have an unexplainable swelling. Or a foot abscess. Or any number of debilitating anomalies which will empty a horse owner's bank account quicker than a stock market crash.

Just last week I went to the barn on Monday to ride my horse who was bright-eyed and energetic as usual. We had a very pleasant ride, after which I washed him off and let him graze for a while in the sun, all the while pondering contentedly how wonderful life with horses was. On Tuesday, I went back out to the barn to ride again. And there stood my horse with a fever, three legs ballooned to the size of elephant limbs, and really gross edema pockets all over his body. What? I backed away, stupefied. What on earth could have happened to transform him overnight into this grotesque image before me?

The usual scenario played out. A vet was called. My horse was treated with every injection medicine available. A diagnosis formed loosely: "Hmm... not really sure what it is. Could have been caused by a tick bite... or an allergy... or who knows. Sometimes this stuff just happens. Call when you need more antibiotics." And that, dear readers, is how my bank account wound its way closer to $0.

I spent the last 10 days driving a total of two hours per day back and forth to the stable to administer drugs and check on my guy. He is fine now. Totally fine, in fact, and back to his normal healthy self. Who knows what caused his episode last week. Must have been a fly bite... or an allergy... or something. One thing's for sure, though. After writing out all those checks to my vet, I wanted to punch the lights out of whoever invented that idiom "healthy as a horse." I would have blurted out, in lunatic fashion, "oh yeah? healthy as a horse? You call this the epitome of health? A creature that can just fall to pieces overnight, possibly from some innocent wildflower blooming?" I think "healthy as a marathon-running octogenarian" might be far more accurate.

My animosity over the idiom settled since last week. I'm no longer screaming out my car window "healthy as a horse?! What crap!" Instead, my mood has turned more reflective, which accounts for my study of these horse-related phrases.

"Horsepower" is another one that mystifies me at the moment. At first, it seems to make sense. I mean, sure, a lawn mower could be called "six horsepower" if it pushed itself along with the strength of six horses in full motion. But this makes the assumption that there is a basic standard for an ordinary horse's power output. As a horse trainer, let me assure you that this is not the case.

How do lawn mower manufacturers, for instance, account for times when horses just aren't putting out any power? Like when a mare comes into heat and flat-out refuses to do anything for three days? Would she be counted as "fussy horsepower" during that period? Or then there's the stall-bound horse recovering from a strained tendon that needs to be confined for three months. Is he counted temporarily as "no horsepower?" Although maybe his tally gets cancelled out by the feisty Arabian who tears around the arena, tail arched over his back, and bucks off his rider every day. Perhaps he gets counted as "one horsepower with spunk to spare?"

You can see how this Horsepower term gets vague. A dozen ornery Shetland ponies will not produce the same output as a dozen steadfast draft horses. And a dozen mares will simply never give a consistent output of agreeable, hormone-free, activity from week to week.

So who came up with this term in the first place? Definitely a non-equestrian. Most likely, an enterprising salesman in a machine shop many moons ago looked out his window and came up with a genius marketing plan. No doubt he looked out at a team of harness horses clip-clopping down the street, lean and muscled and perfectly behaved. Such industrious animals, he probably thought to himself and then pondered how many more engines or motors or machine-like things he could sell if he aligned them with man's good friend, the noble Equine. And, thus, he began equating the capability of his motors and engines with the clip-clopping harness horses he'd seen. A common motorized something-or-other now became a "three horsepower" item. Consumers, therefore, now had all the muscle and brawn of a few horses but without the hay consumption and pooping. Perfect!

Today, I hope most consumers realize how defectively "horsepower" defines what it purports to. For instance, I hope owners of sexy sports cars realize when they rev up their 200 horsepower engines that if, in reality, 200 equines stood at the ready in their driveways, only about ten of them would produce any power. The other 190 would be spooking, grazing, mating, or napping. How's that, for horsepower?

About the Author:

AWARD-WINNING JOURNALIST AND popular instructor Jec A. Ballou was raised by a horse training family in rural New England. She now teaches and trains in Santa Cruz, California where she is also found riding her mountain bike. She is the author of <u>101 Dressage Exercises for Horse and Rider</u> and <u>Equine Fitness: a conditioning program of exercises and routines for your horse</u>, she has spoken at Equine Affaire, Western States Horse Expo, and multiple breed associations.